LIPSTICK WARS

Praise for *Lipstick Wars*

"After reading *Lipstick Wars*, you'll never look at a tube of lipstick in quite the same way. This is a fun page-turner that combines LDS culture, visiting teaching, the challenges of motherhood, and the perils of home ownership all in one makeup bag."
—*Tanya Parker Mills, author of* The Reckoning, *2008 Whitney Finalist and 2009 Indie Book Award Winner for Multicultural Fiction*

"Reading this book is like catching up with friends you haven't seen in a while. A feel-good story of laughing, loving, and learning to cope as an LDS woman. Loved it!"
—*Ann Action, author of* The Miracle Maker

"*Lipstick Wars* explores the complicated dynamics of some of the most powerful people on earth—women—and their capacity to lift or dismantle one another. Christine Thackeray's carefully crafted cast runs the gamut on the perfection scale, becoming entangled in each other's messy lives, and reminding us that compassion and love trump a manicured lawn or immaculately scrubbed kids every time."
—*Laurie C. Lewis, author of* Awakening Avery *and the* Free Men and Dreamer *series*

"Christine Thackeray is able to create characters that we know before we even open the cover of *Lipstick Wars*. They are our neighbors, our visiting teachers, ourselves, and they cope with universal problems: acceptance, misunderstanding, falling short of our own expectations. In laughing at Christine's often hilarious portrayal of the predicaments in which her characters find themselves, we are able to laugh at ourselves. So, *Lipstick Wars* is not only a good read, it's therapeutic."
—*Liz Adair, Whitney Award Winner and best-selling author of* The Mist of Quarry Harbor *and* Counting the Cost

"A charming and funny read for the whole family, sure to tickle the funny bone of anyone who's ever survived a hectic Sunday morning or a crazy neighbor."
—*Michael Young, author of* The Canticle Kingdom

"Christine Thackeray's fun book is not only a witty, entertaining, and insightful read, but also a terrific fashion accessory as you hold it in your hands while sitting by the pool this summer."
—*Trina Boice, author of* Easy Enrichment Ideas, The Ready Resource for Relief Society, *and* Bright Ideas for Young Women Leaders

Lipstick
WARS

Christine Thackeray

Bonneville Books
Springville, Utah

The views expressed within this work are the sole responsibility of the author and do not necessarily reflect the position of Cedar Fort, Inc., or any other entity.

This is a work of fiction. The characters, names, incidents, places, and dialogue are products of the author's imagination, and are not to be construed as real.

ISBN 13: 978-1-59955-391-7

Published by Bonneville Books, an imprint of Cedar Fort, Inc., 2373 W. 700 S., Springville, UT 84663
Distributed by Cedar Fort, Inc., www.cedarfort.com

LIBRARY OF CONGRESS CATALOGING-IN-PUBLICATION DATA

Thackeray, Christine.
   Lipstick wars / Christine Thackeray.
      p. cm.
   Summary: Mormon church members get together and remodel a woman's home so that she and her family won't be evicted.
   ISBN 978-1-59955-391-7
   1. Dwellings--Remodeling--Fiction. 2. Mormons--Fiction. 3. American fiction--21st century. I. Title.
   PS3620.H33L57 2010
   813'.6--dc22
                                        2010005018

Cover design by Danie Romrell
Cover design © 2010 by Lyle Mortimer
Edited and typeset by Melissa J. Caldwell

Printed in the United States of America

10 9 8 7 6 5 4 3 2 1

Printed on acid-free paper

Other books by Christine Thackeray

Could You Be an Angel Today?
C. S. Lewis: Latter-day Truths in Narnia
The Crayon Messages: A Visiting Teaching Adventure

Contents

Contents

Acknowledgments

Goofy Julia Wagner has been my new partner in crime, as we write side by side with children rushing around our feet. She saw things I couldn't. Also, Donna Fuller, the nicest person I know, and her daughter Mandy have endured many chapters in our Enrichment writing group.

I must thank Ellie Gunn, Jina Ortavetz, and Tom Bender, who may not share my faith but definitely share my love of writing. Now they know much more about the Mormon faith than they ever expected to.

Finally, to my dear family for their patience with all the things that are not done and are not done because I have one more chapter I want to finish. Look—it's done!

The Lord answers our prayers, but it is usually through another person that he meets our needs.

–*Spencer W. Kimball*

1

On the Loose

As the police cruiser rolled slowly up the street, Eden stared out the car window, trying not to think about what had just happened. Normally, her neighborhood was like a ghost town. There were evidences of life—huge luxury cars parked in driveways, flowers on doorsteps, and sprinklers watering the unnaturally green front lawns—but rarely had she seen actual people and never out *en masse*. This Sunday morning was different.

Look at them all. She counted at least six neighbors gawking from spacious front yards or peeking out of large bay windows, and by the expressions on their faces, she could tell they had seen everything. One lady with styled auburn hair stood staring by her shiny black Mercedes. She wore a coral outfit with matching lipstick. The woman's thin lips bore amusement coupled with derision at the slow moving squad car.

Eden blinked hard, adjusted the scant towel around her, and hugged her naked toddler, grateful that at least he was safe. She tried not to notice the younger officer in the passenger seat give her a sideways glance and muffle an unexpected chuckle by clearing his throat.

Averting her eyes, Eden caught sight of her closest neighbor, Mrs. Murdock, who was standing in her immaculate doorway with hands on her hips, nodding in approval. A floppy straw gardening hat shaded her piercing eyes, but the disdain was clear enough. *So she called again.* The last few times Murdock had phoned the police, it had seemed cruel and humiliating, but today Eden was almost grateful—almost. She vowed to think nicer thoughts about the retired math teacher in the future.

Eden could see the high broad fence at the end of the road come into view. The padlock and chain across its gate seemed a symbol of her personal prison. Behind the fence, she gazed at the land still wild and undeveloped. Ironically, even it looked better cared for than the shabby hovel she called home.

"It's here, on the left—the old Victorian." She broke the silence as the older officer nodded and gave a meaningful look to his partner.

Her house had been the original homestead of the surrounding development and was probably beautiful at the turn of the century— the last century. Time and a coat of faded blue paint the color of tacky eye shadow hid its traditional charm. The front porch was sagging and covered with plastic Little Tykes ride-on toys from garage sales. She had hoped Hayden would play on them as soon as the waist-high lawn got under control, but last week Josh had bent his third lawn mower blade after only one pass. The lawn mower sat trapped in the middle of the untamed front yard, advertising its ineptness. The scene made her think of a few redneck jokes, and she could hardly believe she lived there herself.

The officers had attempted to be respectful as they drove past the upscale properties that lined her neighborhood—Hummer Homes, her mother called them, expensive but poorly built. But Eden noticed their expressions change once they saw where she lived. They pulled into her cracked driveway, and she sank in her seat.

Her husband, Josh, was leisurely loading the baby into the car for church. Slung over his shoulder was a diaper bag stuffed so full that it looked like a pair of too tight jeans on a Weight Watchers flunky. Eden stared at the bag and bit her lip. *He's trying to be nice. He's trying.* Eden wanted to feel grateful, she really did, but under the circumstances, she couldn't stir up any of those emotions. Every other feeling was drowned out by the fact that he was supposed to have been watching Hayden while she showered.

She waited for one of the officers to open her door and stood directly before her husband with only a towel wrapped around her and her naked two-year-old son in her arms. The shock on his face at seeing them both undressed was blatant. "Wow, I bet you guys gave the entire neighborhood an eyeful. No wonder they called the police."

"Very funny. And yes, I think the whole neighborhood did see me.

I didn't catch him until we were almost to the highway." Eden stopped herself from lashing out with blame, shoved Hayden in his already filled arms, and turned to the older officer who had just emerged from the car. "Am I permitted to go inside and dress, sir?"

"That would be fine." He nodded, and Eden rushed toward the house.

Behind her she could hear her husband say, "You have to admit he is becoming quite the escape artist. He even escaped from his clothes this time."

She cringed, slammed the door, and hurried to the bedroom. *Josh always cracks jokes when he's nervous. Doesn't he understand that those men aren't friends?* She slipped her soft taupe-colored dress over her head and pulled it down into place. *They're here to investigate us—to judge if we're good parents. This is serious.*

Eden took a deep breath and tried to calm herself. She could hear laughing in the front room and knew she'd better get in there before Josh said something he shouldn't. He was a loving and good-hearted man—that's why she had married him—but he wasn't very careful with how he presented himself or their family.

As she turned to rush out the door, she caught her reflection in the mirror. Her pale skin looked taut and haggard. Her hair had dried frizzy and uncontrolled. Although Eden knew she should hurry back to the officers, something in her couldn't do it.

Walking back to the bathroom, she lifted the brush to her hair, plugged in the straightener, and reached under the sink for her makeup bag. She laid the sleek leather case on the yellowed counter and unrolled it. A collection of brushes, applicators, and small containers of every shape and color glistened in the cramped bathroom.

Hurriedly, she pulled out her bronzer and brush as her mind drifted to the families in the ward that seemed so perfect. She thought about Cath Reed, who always sat on the second row at church with her husband and four beautiful children. They were all so well-behaved and happy. She imagined their family was already sitting in their seats listening to the prelude music. Her eyes flicked back to the door where she knew the policemen waited. *Why can't my life be more like hers?*

Twelve minutes later, Eden put on a layer of berry nut lipstick, lifted her chin, and relaxed her shoulders. Now the mirror reflected a polished young woman exuding confidence. Eden swallowed, hoping that was all the officers would see. Then, taking a deep breath, she walked out of the room with as bright a smile as she could muster.

· · · · ·

A dented sedan crept past the high-end development to the back of the cul-de-sac and came to an abrupt halt. The car door groaned open, revealing a foot clad in a dingy bathroom slipper. The disheveled woman shuffled forward and slid her ornate key in the crusted lock with a paint-stained hand. After much protesting, the lock gave way.

Charred skeletal remains of the old mansion loomed above decades of overgrowth in the distance, dwarfing the simple box-shaped garage apartment, the last standing structure of the once grand estate. No one had opened the locked wrought iron gates or climbed the winding gravel path to its doors for years until this Sunday morning, and her heart filled with dread at the prospect.

As she walked back to her car, the woman's gaze drifted to her left where a cozy blue cottage that held her fondest memories seemed teeming with life. Her brow furrowed as she noticed the squad car out front, and she flicked her gaze across the street to the colorless tract home that stood facing it in sterile defiance. Her thick, unevenly drawn deep red lips pulled flat in what was intended to be a smile but looked more like a grimace. "So you want a war, do you?" she whispered before climbing back in her car and roaring up the driveway to her new home.

2

A Missionary Haircut

ess than a mile away, Cath Reed sat in front of her computer chewing on the nub of a pencil.

"Mom, I'm all dressed. Now can you cut my hair? I look like a skater, and I want to look like a missionary to match my new outfit, see?" Mike stood up straight and lifted his chin to show off his tie, white shirt, and well-cut navy blue suit.

"I know, I know, but I have one more sentence, and I'll have this talk finished. Why don't you get out the clippers and towel? We'll squeeze it in before we have to leave for church, I promise." Cath typed the final few words and pushed the print button.

Kevin had told her they were assigned to speak in sacrament meeting three weeks ago. The first two weeks were spent getting everyone's rooms organized and the back-to-school shopping done. Add basic procrastination to the mix, and getting her talk prepared wasn't even on her to-do list.

Last week school had began, and Kevin was out of town again. Every day held some type of emergency. Carson got new glasses and broke both pairs. Sandra forgot her math book, and Mike lost his lunch money. Saturday was Jordan's first football game, and it wasn't until late that night when they walked through the front door, starving and exhausted, that her husband, the executive secretary, reminded her of the speaking assignment. Cath wanted to smack him when he smugly admitted to having prepared his talk two weeks earlier.

By the time she had collapsed in bed last night, the hope of her mind coming up with anything intelligent to say had completely vanished, so Cath planned to wake up early and pull together her thoughts. After helping her husband get out the door two hours earlier, she had finally sat at the computer ready to face her assigned topic, integrity.

If she had been uninterrupted, she might have finished in half an hour, but Carson and Jordan had been fighting over the kids' computer, which they weren't even supposed to be playing on, and Mike had been in at least five times asking for a haircut. It didn't matter that all summer she had begged him to let her cut it when she had the time. Now that it was Sunday morning, and she didn't have the time, it was an emergency.

Cath watched the pages as they spit out of the printer. Suddenly, she had a funny feeling and looked up at the clock. Her face fell. "Sandra, Jordan, Carson, Mike, we only have twenty-three minutes before we have to be there!" Running up the stairs, she called again, "Hurry. Get dressed and brush your teeth. I can't be late."

As she rushed past Sandra's door, she noticed it was closed. Turning the handle, Cath took a tentative step into the darkness before flicking on the light.

"Off, now!" the voice demanded under the rumpled quilt.

Cath looked around the room littered with clothes, books, towels, and shoes. "It's time to get up, honey, and this room is out of control. When you get home from church, why don't you work on it?"

"I thought this was supposed to be a day of rest." Sandra brought the comforter down to her nose, exposing her cropped blonde hair. Her eyes barely squinted open. "Do you really want me to break the rules? Because if you do—"

"Fine, I'm not going to argue with you. I'm speaking today and need to be on time. You have the choice to come dressed or in your PJ's, but you don't have the choice not to come. We're leaving in fifteen minutes." Cath walked out of the room, willing herself to let it go. Lately, between Sandra leaving so early for seminary and getting in late with sports, the girl was hardly home, and then she was usually on the phone. It seemed like the few conversations they did have always ended in an argument. When they talked, Cath felt like she was making her way through a field of land mines. One wrong step and everything could blow up in her face.

Cath closed her door and jumped in the shower, scrubbing her hair and soaping up at the same time. She didn't hear the door open and her six-year-old son walk into the room.

"Mom, aren't you going to cut my hair?" Mike pleaded. "I need it cut really bad."

Cath turned off the water and stuck her head out from behind the shower curtain. "Honey, I'm really sorry. I know I said I would, but we're going to be late. Just gel it, and I'll cut it after church. It'll look fine. Now, can you let Mom have some private time to get ready, please?"

Mike left with his shoulders drooping and his head bowed. Cath felt awful but didn't know what else to do. She threw on a towel and rushed into her room to find the door wide open with Carson and Jordan picking through the laundry basket filled with unmatched socks at the foot of her bed.

"Ew, Mom. Get some clothes on," Jordan said.

"At least I'm not wearing my glasses," joked Carson.

"Uh, I believe this is my room, and I'm trying to get dressed if you don't mind." The boys headed out as Sandra dashed in and ran for the bathroom.

"Mom, I just have to grab a few things." Sandra was wearing layered tees and a brown knit skirt.

"I'm just happy to see you getting ready." While Cath rummaged through her drawers in search of a pair of nylons that weren't run, Sandra hurried out of the room. Cath threw on her black skirt with a fresh white blouse and bright green jacket. She dried her hair and touched up the front. Pulling open her makeup drawer, she froze. It had been robbed.

"Sandra, come in here!"

Her teenage daughter stuck her head in the door with the most innocent look on her face that Cath had ever seen. "What do you want?"

"Where did all my makeup go?"

"I only took what was mine."

"What do you mean? There is no mascara. I had three of them yesterday. The only blush you left me is bright orange, and there are only two tubes of lipstick left, deep red and salmon."

"The salmon matches the blush." The vengeful grin on her daughter's face was not lost on Cath.

"I don't have time for this. Bring me your makeup kit, and we'll divvy up the stuff later."

"You can't steal my makeup. That's not fair."

"We can talk about what's fair later. Now, just do it. We've only got . . ." Cath looked at the clock. "EIGHT MINUTES!"

Sandra marched from the room as Cath put away the toothpaste, hairbrush, and blow dryer and rushed into the closet to slip on her shoes.

"Here it is, Mom." Sandra dumped the shoebox-sized Tupperware container on the counter and stood at the door. "Can I at least drive this morning?"

"Great idea. You need the hours, and if I get behind the wheel, there is no way I won't speed like a crazy lady. Why don't you grab the boys and pile them in the car? I'll be down in two minutes, promise."

"Do I have to do everything?" Sandra stomped away.

Cath looked at the plastic bin overflowing with all sorts of lip gloss, blush, and shadow. She dusted her cheeks, passed a mascara wand across her lashes, and dabbed on a little lip gloss before dashing down the stairs.

Within minutes Sandra was adjusting the rearview mirror. She looked over her shoulder and eased the gearshift out of park. Cath tried to distract herself so she wouldn't make her daughter nervous. It was three minutes before the hour but a seven-minute drive to church. They would be late, but she would still be there in plenty of time to speak. She glanced back at the three boys and gasped.

"Mike, what happened to your hair?" It was gelled straight down and brushed flat, but it looked like he had tried to trim his bangs straight. The bowl cut made him look as goofy as Jim Cary in *Dumb and Dumber*. Cath reached back and pushed his bangs to the side, exposing a large bald spot about the size of a quarter right at the front of his hairline.

"Oh my heck!" Cath screeched.

Sandra threw on the brakes, making everyone jerk forward. The car behind them squealed to a stop inches from their bumper. "What's wrong?! Did I hit something?"

"I'm sorry," Cath said, catching her breath. "We've got to turn around."

Sandra was shaking from the scare. She waited for the other driver to pass her before turning back toward the house.

"Whoa, dude, what'd you do?" asked Carson.

Mike's bottom lip began to quiver. "I wanted a missionary haircut so I cut it, but it looked bad. I thought you wouldn't notice."

Carson laughed. "News flash. We noticed."

"It's okay." Jordan put an arm around his little brother. "You should've seen the time I gave Carson a haircut. Now that was funny. Mom had to totally shave him bald."

"I was eighteen months old and practically bald anyway," Carson shot back as they pulled in the driveway. "And I looked cool bald!"

Cath threw the car door open as Sandra was still coming to a stop. "Come on, Mike. I'm so sorry, honey. Let's give you that missionary haircut right now."

When they finally got back in the car, Cath was racing down the road well over the speed limit while Sandra clung on for dear life in the passenger seat. Mike sat in the back next to his two brothers, toting what looked far more like a military haircut than a missionary one, and at home, on the tray of the printer, sat the only copy of Cath's sacrament meeting talk.

3

Putting Up a Good Front

"So, let me get this straight," the older officer said, looking at his notes. "You saw your son from the window and ran out the door in nothin' but your skivvies so you could catch him. But why didn't you ask your husband to do it? He was here at the time, wasn't he?"

"I tried. I yelled for him twice, but he didn't answer." Eden stood up and took the fussy baby from Josh, hoping she would have more success in calming Miley down. It was half an hour past her feeding time, but Eden knew she couldn't leave, and there was no way she was going to breast-feed in front of these men—they had seen too much already.

Josh opened his mouth to interject but did a double-take and sprang across the room to catch Hayden in the last stages of his second striptease act of the morning. "That's the problem with Pull-Ups. They pull down way too easily." Josh blew a raspberry into his son's exposed belly, and Hayden giggled. Then he sat on the ground, wrestling his young son's clothes back on while flipping him over his shoulder and upside down.

Eden rolled her eyes and scowled. She wanted to tell Josh that he had to correct Hayden, not reward him for his bad behavior, but she didn't dare say the words in front of the officers.

Miley was quickly escalating from fussing to truly crying, and Eden tried to comfort her, patting the infant in rhythmic taps. She turned to the policemen seriously, trying to get back on the subject. "Don't you understand? I couldn't wait another second. Hayden was already halfway down the street. I had to go."

The younger officer spoke up in an attempt to be heard over the whining baby. "But why would the kid run away like that? Were you fighting?"

Eden recoiled. "Of course not. We never fight."

She bent down and began yanking things out of the overfilled diaper bag in search of a pacifier while bouncing the noisy baby up and down on her shoulder. She pulled out a tub of Vaseline, three bottles of baby shampoo, the toothbrush kit she had gotten from the hospital, and a full box of Cheerios and threw them on the couch. "What were you thinking when you packed all this stuff?" Eden hissed at her husband under her breath and bent over to continue to rifle through the bag.

The officer pursed his lips at his partner and then looked at Eden. "Well, you said you yelled at your husband—twice. Maybe the kid thought you were fighting."

Eden found the pacifier, put it gently in her baby's mouth, and then turned to face them. "Look, do either of you have children?"

Both men shook their heads.

Eden swallowed and paused. *They have no clue what I'm attempting to accomplish here. It's like talking to my mother!* She spoke slowly, trying to get them to understand. "Hayden has just become mobile, and we're struggling with teaching him limits. It's been a learning curve, but we have things under control." Each word of the last sentence spit from her mouth in frustration.

"Things didn't look under control when we picked you up," the younger officer shot back.

"We are doing our best." She paced the floor and, catching sight of the front hall, spun around to face them again. "Just look at that door. We have a chain, a dead bolt, and a childproof cover on the doorknob!"

"Yup," Josh added from his seat in the corner, "it's a real Fort Knox."

Eden took a step forward, pleading. "Can't you just forgive us this once? It will never happen again. I promise. We are doing the best we can." She felt on the verge of something awful and stared at them as her words hung silently in the air.

Both men looked at her with straight expressions, and then the older one softened. "You seem like good parents and all, but our hands are tied. It's a third offense, and we've already reported in. The state will have to get involved."

Eden shook her head, unwilling to believe what she was hearing. "The first time Hayden was still in the front yard. This is normal behavior . . . for him. If it wasn't for our neighbor who sits around all day watching us, trying to find the smallest thing wrong and calling the police at the drop of a hat . . ."

They would not meet her eyes. "You can tell that to Family Services. They'll figure it out," said the older officer, trying to calm her down. "Someone should be contacting you in the next few days. We'll see ourselves out."

Josh jumped up and opened the door for them. "Come again, anytime." He waved and smiled to them with Hayden in his arms mimicking his every move. When they were gone, he turned confidently to Eden. "Well, I think that went well."

She bit her lip and closed her eyes. "What are you talking about?"

"They said we were good parents. It'll be fine."

Miley spit out her pacifier and let out a yell that mirrored Eden's feelings exactly.

*   *   *   *   *

Dropping her hand from the slats of her front blinds, Helen Murdock hurried out the door and down the walk. "Officers, is everything all right? That poor little family."

"Fine, fine." The older officer had his car door open and put his foot up on the running board.

"Is there anything I can do to help? I am the president of the homeowners' association." The woman clutched her straw hat in her hands across her heart.

"No, it's just too bad we had to turn them into the state," the younger policeman mused. "They seem like nice people."

"How horrible." Helen covered her mouth in feigned disbelief.

"I wouldn't worry about it, ma'am. I'm sure everything will be fine. It's standard procedure, but I doubt anything will come of it."

Helen placed her hat securely on her head and stood bone straight, watching the squad car pull away before marching up the street to gather more ammunition. "Not if I have anything to say about it."

4
Not Getting What You Want

By the time they finally made it to church, Miley was completely hysterical—too upset to eat. Eden didn't even get to think about going in the chapel and headed right for the mother's lounge, while Miley screamed with frantic hiccups and would not be comforted.

At last the baby fell asleep on Eden's shoulder, hiccupping, covered with sweat, and still unfed. Although Eden knew it was temporary, she knew she needed something. The events of the morning had left her so empty inside. Even if she could only catch a few minutes of Gospel Doctrine, it would be worth it. She had heard the bell and knew that Josh would be teaching the teenagers and Hayden would be in nursery, so Eden went straight for the cultural hall.

As she began to open the cultural hall door, she heard a bang behind her and turned in time to see Hayden run out of the nursery undetected and hide deep in the coat rack. *This is too much*, she thought, trying to stem her rising anger. She grabbed her son's arm and dragged him back to the nursery as quickly and silently as she could so as not to wake the baby.

Hillary Jacobs, the new nursery leader, rushed over to Eden and Hayden as soon as she spotted them, announcing, "Now where did you take yourself off to, little man?" Eden gave half a smile and turned to leave, but Hillary cut her off. "So this is the baby! Can I see her?"

With a finger to her lips, Eden shook her head, hoping Hillary would get the hint. The woman, blind to subtlety, reached out and took the sleeping infant off her mother's shoulder.

Miley wailed in sudden awareness, and Hillary laughed. "I'm not that bad, am I?"

Frustrated that any hope of actually attending a meeting that day was quickly flying out the window, Eden tried to be polite. "I'll take her, Hillary. Just keep a better eye on Hayden, okay?" The words came out sharper than she intended, and Eden regretted it the minute they had escaped her mouth.

Hillary put the screaming baby back in her mother's arms. "Well, I'm not the one who raised him, am I?" She began putting away toys, violently slamming them in their respective baskets and bins.

Eden opened her mouth to reply, but Miley's screams silenced her. She ducked out the door and returned to the mother's lounge for sanctuary.

Half an hour later, Eden was still there, singing sweetly to her happy baby who had been fed and changed.

> *I know a girl who name is Miley,*
> *Hey la-dee-la-dee-o,*
> *When she's fed, she cute and smiley,*
> *Hey la-dee-la-dee-o.*

The door flew open with a thud that made Eden jump. A surprised teenage girl paused for a second but then closed the door and sat in the soft chair across from her. "Do you mind if I hide out here for a second? The Sunday School lesson is so boring that I think I'm going to die."

Eden shrugged and continued to hum to her baby as she finished packing up the crowded bag.

"What's that song?" The cute blonde teenager smiled. "I know it. I think we learned it at girl's camp this year. You sing camp songs to your baby?" She wrinkled her nose.

"Well, sometimes. Besides, girl's camp was where I was first introduced to the gospel."

"Really? I'm Sandra, by the way. Sandra Reed."

"Oh, you're one of the Reeds? Your family is so awesome."

"You don't know us very well, do you?" Sandra twirled in her chair aimlessly. "So girl's camp is where you joined the Church?"

"In a way." Eden sat down and rocked the baby. "The summer before my junior year in high school, a friend invited me to go. I knew nothing about the Church, but I wanted to spend time with her, so I went."

Sandra kicked off her flats and sat cross-legged in the soft arm chair, tucking her skirt down. "That's how old I am. Was she your best friend?"

"It's more like her whole family was my best friend. In eighth grade the Clawsons moved in across the street. Actually, they kind of invaded the neighborhood. There were ten in their family."

"Sheesh. I thought we had a houseful with six."

"I'd never met such a big family in my life. I didn't even know it was possible to have that many kids, but it was wonderful. My mom worked really long hours, so I had spent a lot of time alone, but from day one it was like they adopted me. I ended up spending almost every day at their house for those three years."

"Wasn't it noisy and crowded?"

"That was the beauty of it." Eden found a smile floating to her lips as she recalled that happy time. "Somewhere among the food fights, huge laundry piles, and having bubble wars in the kitchen sink on Robin's dish day, I decided that's what I wanted more than anything in the whole world—a big, bustling, happy family."

Sandra ran her finger around the edge of the chair. "Well, I come from a pretty big family, and it's not all it's cracked up to be."

"I know what you mean." Eden's mind drifted back to the events of the morning. "It's a lot harder than I ever imagined, and I only have two." She wondered if she was really capable of it all.

Just then Miley cooed gently in the silence. The sound of the content baby charmed the teenager. Sandra stood and took a hesitant step toward them. "Can I hold her? She really is beautiful."

Eden handed Miley to her, and for a few minutes both women stared, transfixed by the innate powerful draw of the precious infant. The noises in the hall suddenly increased. "I better get going. Young Women is starting." She handed back the baby. "But if ever you need a babysitter, I'm game."

Eden watched the door close like a great tide receding and knew that she could never leave her kids with someone, especially while Hayden was acting like a fugitive. *It's odd that the part of the gospel that hooked me was that families could be forever. It's all I've wanted for so long.*

Her gaze dropped to the ground. *No one ever told me it'd be so hard and lonely.*

Miley began squirming, and Eden pulled the baby closer to her and took a step toward the door. She stumbled slightly and looked down to find Sandra's canvas flats lying across each other at her feet beside the chair. *Even Sandra's mom, Cath, has it all together, and she has twice as many kids as I do.* She stuck Sandra's shoes in the outside pocket of her bag. *It's like I'm not good enough. I just can't do it.*

A lump seemed to grow in her throat. *Maybe Mom's right that in today's world having a big family isn't possible.* Eden recalled their conversation the day before. "Listen, Eden, how are you going to afford raising all these babies when you don't have a degree yourself? The minute you come back to your senses and decide to go back to school, I'll cover your daycare costs."

Less than twenty-four hours ago the words were abhorrent to her, but now Eden wondered. *Maybe Mom's right, and two is all I can handle.* Her eyes drifted down to the baby. Miley caught her mother's gaze and beamed at her, exposing hidden dimples on her chin and left cheek.

Eden felt warm inside and bent down to kiss her baby but stopped herself, not wanting to dirty her daughter's perfect face with her lipstick. Still, she couldn't help but smile back. But that smile quickly dimmed when she noticed the door open a crack. Hayden peeked at his mother through the little space between the door and frame. *I wonder if Hillary let him out intentionally for spite.*

Taking a deep breath to contain herself, she sneaked up to the door, hoping not to startle him until he was within arm's reach. The moment he realized what was happening, Hayden laughed wildly and dashed away. Eden shook her head, grabbed the diaper bag, and, with Miley in her arms, headed out to go catch her little Houdini again.

5

Casting Lots

Josh saved her.

"You up for trading places?" He greeted her in the hall as she headed for the nursery the second time with Hayden screaming in tow. He took Miley with one arm and grabbed Hayden with the other.

"Really?" Eden smiled in gratitude and relief. "You're the greatest, Josh." Looking at the clock on the wall, she knew if she hurried she might only miss the opening prayer.

Eden couldn't remember the last time she had sat through a Relief Society lesson. Between serving in Primary and having the babies, it had been at least two years. She hoped it was a lesson on motherhood, coping with stress, or maybe even on the eternal nature of families. What she wanted to hear more than anything were the words, "You're doing a good job." She wanted to be reminded that it was all worth it and that she was doing the most important work of eternity because right now she only felt exhausted with no rest or end in sight.

Hoping to be filled and lifted, she opened the door but silence struck her. The room was empty. Eden couldn't believe it. She was sure this was the Relief Society room; after all, it said so on the door. Dejected by the discovery, she decided to go home early when Brenda Ramsey, the Relief Society president, rushed in, unlocked the closet door, and snatched up some brightly colored napkins.

"Oh, Eden, what are you doing in here? We're in the cultural hall, and my goodness, do we need you. Come on." Sister Ramsey put an arm around Eden, and before Eden knew it, she was whisked into the gym.

Round tables had been set up close to the front with three black-boards on wheels acting as screens to enclose the group. Almost every chair was filled. Most of the other women Eden knew were in Primary and sat in a cluster at the far side of the gym. Brenda led her to an empty chair and motioned her to sit with a group of three women. Two of them she had never seen before, and the other was Cath, Sandra's mom. Then Sister Ramsey ran up to the front and began talking.

"I'm sorry we're starting late, sisters. We are so happy to have you here at our visiting teaching conference. We got special permission to have it during this last hour, so we could get as many of you here as possible. I mean, let's face it, if we were to have it on a Saturday, we may only get me here—oh, and maybe Cath over there, but that's about it."

Cath laughed, and the tan woman beside her tapped her friend's arm in jest, making the gold bangles around her wrist jingle against her coral sleeve. Eden's face turned pink as she realized she had seen this woman before from the window of the police cruiser that morning. She knew the woman had recently moved into the ward but had no idea she lived down the street from her. The color of the outfit was unmistakable, and Eden began to feel hot with shame, remembering the look of amusement on the woman's thin lips as the police car passed. Eden looked down and turned her chair toward the speaker, hoping her neighbor wouldn't recognize her.

Eden's attention wandered to the young woman who sat beside her. She had moved into the ward about the same time as her neighbor. Eden didn't think this sister and her husband had any children—at least she didn't look like she had kids. Her figure was perfect, and she always appeared professional with every hair in place.

Today she was wearing an expensive black silk suit that matched her gleaming ebony hair pulled into a simple gold clip. Her lips were the same color as the small handkerchief peeking from her pocket and her bright cherry stilettos. Eden imagined the woman was close to her age, but she looked so much more mature than Eden ever felt. She tried to smile at her, but the woman turned her face forward with an annoyed expression.

The Relief Society president continued. "Sisters, if I could do one thing in this world, it would be to have you really understand the great need for visiting teaching. On the outside the women around you may look like their lives are totally together, but inside many of the sisters in our ward are desperate. They are desperate for help in coping with their lives, desperate for friendship, desperate to feel the Spirit.

"Many sisters around you are praying daily that the Lord will send someone to help them. And you know what? He has. He's sent you. Sisters, I challenge you to be the kind of visiting teachers who make a difference. To truly love those you visit and become the answer to their prayers."

Eden found a stray tear rolling down her cheek and embarrassingly whisked it away. She hoped that the president's words could in fact be true for one second, but then reality set in. Since she had been married five years ago, she had seen her visiting teachers exactly twice—once when she first moved into the ward and once when she had Hayden. They hadn't even come in, just stood on the doorstep and left flowers.

When she and Josh moved from their apartment into the house last year and when Miley was born, no one had even done that. She guessed people thought they were young and strong and didn't need the help.

Eden noticed a funny expression on Sister Ramsey's face like she was nervous about what she was saying, and Eden listened more intently. "All right, I know this is unconventional. You see, I had all the routes set up last night, and I kept feeling gray inside like something was terribly wrong. Then right before we went to bed, my husband said he wanted to read the scriptures with me. Now, if you know Bill, that is a miracle in and of itself. I don't think he has ever been one to want to read the Book of Mormon together—ever. So who was I to say no?

"Well, he turned to a place in first Nephi where Nephi and his brothers were deciding who would go up to Laban to try to get the brass plates. Although Nephi was willing to go, he felt he should cast lots to give his brothers the opportunity. This idea seemed to make me tingle all over. Although I did the routes, I thought that for the next quarter, your companion and routes could be chosen by casting lots. If you look around the room, I have you sitting at tables with even numbers. There is a plate in front of you. Would everyone please turn over your plate?"

Eden did as instructed, but her plate was blank. Cath and the younger professional woman both looked at the lists glued to the bottom of their plates. The room began to fill with chatter. Brenda continued loudly, "If you have a plate with writing on it, then the person to your left is your companion, and the names on your list are the women you visit teach."

Looking around doubtfully, Eden bit at her thumbnail. There were no place cards anywhere. How could random assignments possibly be inspired? Feeling more hopeless than ever, she dropped her hands to her lap and glanced over to see the two women across the table, laughing and gabbing like old friends. Cath squealed and turned to Eden's neighbor with her perfectly styled hair, full makeup job, and manicured nails. "Marlene, you're my companion, and," she pointed to the younger woman on Eden's right, "Kimberly, we visit teach you and a lady named Eden Duncan. Do you know Eden Duncan, Marlene?"

"She must be in the Primary clique. Those ladies are such snobs. They won't talk to anyone who doesn't have snot on their shoulders." Marlene clicked her tongue, shooting a furtive glare across the room.

Eden swallowed, wanting to make a quick exit but blurted out softly, "It's me."

Cath gawked at her in surprise. "What are the chances of that happening? Wow. So I guess you and Kimberly are companions." Kimberly looked at Eden with less enthusiasm than Eden felt herself. She guessed that the woman's suit cost more than her entire wardrobe, and those red shoes were definitely a designer brand.

Putting a hand over the wet spot on her shoulder where her sleeping baby had been, Eden tried to act confident. "So who do we have?"

"This must be a mistake," Kimberly said with a businesslike tone. She stood and strode over to Sister Ramsey. After a brief discussion, she returned with a disgusted look on her face. "You are not going to believe this. Eden, is it? We have those two." She jabbed a manicured finger in the direction of Cath and Marlene. "This is ridiculous. It doesn't make any sense."

Cath laughed. "You mean you aren't happy about it? We can do our visiting teaching while we walk in the morning; it'll be great. We'll get 100 percent with our eyes closed."

Kimberly shook her head angrily. "That is if Eden here wants to go walking with us, which I very much doubt."

"Well, I might be able to make it. Where do you walk?" Eden's stomach tightened for even mentioning it. The last thing she needed was more to do, and there was no way she could leave her children, especially with Hayden being so out of control.

Marlene Thomas was looking bored and took out her nail file to buff the tiniest imperfection off her shiny coral two-inch nails. "We walk in Timberlake. Both Kimberly and I live there, and Cath here lives right around the corner in one of the *older* houses."

Marlene never looked up, but the way she said "older houses" made Eden's already unhappy stomach do flip-flops. She wondered what Marlene would think of her house. The one good thing was that it was obvious the woman hadn't recognized her. Eden felt relieved.

Kimberly sat down and folded her hands out on the table in front of her like a hanging judge. "So where do you live?" She stared at Eden, expecting a response.

Seconds seemed like minutes as Eden tried to think of a way to avoid answering. She wanted to change the subject. She wanted to curl up and die. She wanted to run away and never come back, but she felt there was nothing else she could do; they would find out soon enough. "I live in Timberlake too—in the little Victorian at the end of the street," she unwillingly confessed for the second time that day.

Marlene suddenly looked up and lifted her perfectly arched eyebrows. "You live in the *shack*?"

Cath gave her uncouth friend a censuring look and turned to Eden. "Wow, that's your house? We pass by it every morning. It has a lot of potential."

Cath's words were meant to be nice but stung. Eden took deep breaths so she wouldn't start crying.

Marlene's mouth was still open as she stared closely at Eden through squinted eyes. She smirked and sat back in her chair triumphantly. "Well, I know that Eden likes to walk. As a matter of fact, she was out running this morning, weren't you?"

Eden silently pleaded that she wouldn't say more.

At last, Kimberly slapped her hands on the table. "Fine. Walking group it is. We'll pick you up at six o'clock sharp. If you aren't out front, we keep going."

Eden nodded, confused about when she had agreed to be part of this. But before she could say anything else, Sister Ramsey asked for everyone's attention. They ended with a song and a prayer. The minute they said "Amen," Hayden came bursting through the door, followed by her husband holding a fussy Miley. Eden listened to her little boy babble about his crayon picture while Josh handed her the baby, told her he had to return something to the library, and shot out of the room.

By the time Eden looked around, the other women at her table had left. She let it go, excited to socialize with her friends from Primary and show off the new baby. Heather and Erin, both in the Primary presidency, were talking animatedly to each other in a tight group. She walked over to them and stood, waiting for a break in the conversation. Not noticing her, they hurried out the door, still discussing the activity they were planning. Eden stood alone in the crowded room. She swallowed and took Hayden's hand, wishing she hadn't come.

6

One Step at a Time

The water suddenly shot out scalding hot, and Eden screamed in spite of herself. She poked her head out behind the new embroidered shower curtain, her only improvement in the bathroom since they'd moved there. "Josh, you aren't supposed to flush the toilet while I'm in here. You know that!"

"Sorry, Eden, but I don't think that's a habit you want me to break. At least I put down the toilet seat for you." Josh smiled and turned on the faucet to wash his hands. The stream of water spraying from the rusted showerhead slowed to a trickle, and Eden twisted the yellowed crystal handles of the antique tub to the off position and grabbed her towel, huffing in protest.

"What are you doing taking a shower now anyway? It's not even five in the morning." He shook his hands in the air, wiped them off on the rear of his pajama pants, and began walking back to the warm bed. "I thought you said that the walking group didn't start until about six—that's over an hour and a half away."

Eden finished drying off behind the shower curtain. "I had to get up to feed the baby anyway, and if I laid back down, I'd probably fall asleep."

"I thought that was the idea," Josh answered through a yawn.

"You know how long it takes me to get ready in the morning, and I can't be late. After all, what would they think of me? I don't know these women yet, so I really have to make a good impression."

Josh flopped on the bed, leaving the heavy oak door open between them. "I'm worried. You just had a baby, and with Hayden's little jaunts, are you sure this won't be too much? You don't have to be Superwoman, you know."

How could he say that? she thought as she whipped the towel snugly around her. *Superwoman? I'm just the opposite. I'm never caught up on laundry, I can't keep the toys put away and oh, I'm being investigated by the state for being a bad mother—Superwoman!* She glowered at him from behind the shower curtain and then yanked it back with a dramatic tug. The weak plaster holding up the rod gave way, and the entire bar, rings, and curtain fell to the black and white tiled floor with a loud clank.

"You don't have to be the Incredible Hulk either," he said, laughing with his head still on the pillow.

Eden knelt down, gathered up the entire mess, and stuffed it in the tub. She tried not to think about this being one more thing to do on an ever-growing list. Somewhere in the back of her head she could hear her mother's words echo, "That house will be a chain around your neck," but she couldn't forget the warm feeling she had when she first walked in the door.

From the outside she had turned up her nose at the house and didn't even want to walk in, but as she stepped into the large front room, an assurance engulfed her that she immediately recognized. Josh felt it too, and two weeks later, they were signing papers.

It was terrible timing. With the pregnancy she couldn't do as much as she normally would, so they were still only half moved in. Even now, looking at the gaping holes she had created on either side of the tub, she knew Heavenly Father wanted her here. *Maybe it's to test me,* she thought and hurried through the bedroom and toward the closet to dress.

•   •   •   •   •

"Hey, they'll be here in five minutes," Josh said dreamily with one eye open looking at the clock. He turned and sat up. "You're still getting ready? I think that's a record even for you." He rolled over and threw the pillow over his head, trying to block out the light.

Eden couldn't believe how fast the time had gone by and slapped on her new lipstick that changed shades depending on the lip liner you she used. She bared her teeth in the mirror to make sure they were perfectly white and swiftly tucked her makeup back away. Dashing into the bedroom, she grabbed Josh's pillow and kissed him on the forehead, leaving a big pinkish spot that looked a little like a bruise. "Are you sure you can handle this? It's going to be tough getting ready and watching the kids."

Josh smiled and rolled over. "You may not be Superwoman, but I'm Superman. I can handle anything life throws at me—anything." Eden couldn't resist and threw the pillow at his head.

Josh kicked his feet up under the covers and gave a dramatic wounded moan. "You got me."

She hurried out into the hall and pulled her husband's Nike pants higher around her waist, tightening the drawstring on the inside. She had changed three times before finally deciding to wear them. All of her cute exercise clothes didn't quite fit since she had the baby. *It's a good thing I'm going walking after all,* she told herself.

Eden undid the chain and bolt and opened the front door tentatively. She gasped. For the second time since she had moved here, the street was swarming with people. After carefully locking the door behind her, she hurried to the curb and began pretending to stretch while gaping at the relatively busy road. She had thought Sunday morning there were a lot of people, but there were even more now. During the day there seemed to be no one around except for Mrs. Murdock, who she tried to stay as far away from as possible.

Four old men wearing shorts and dark socks tramped by in unison, engulfed in serious conversation. Eden couldn't help but laugh. There were two other groups of women, one of which looked like they were training for a marathon—three thin, tan, muscle-bound professionals in sports bras and tiny shorts to flaunt their perfect bodies. She adjusted the baggy sweats and watched a pair of older women on their way back toward the nice side of the street. They seemed far more interested in exercising their mouths than their legs.

It wasn't long before Eden noticed a tall slender figure coming toward her with two shorter women struggling to keep up. At the front, Kimberly set the pace for the other two. Marlene was at her heels with her taut chin held high as they walked, clenching her jaw to make the exertion appear effortless. Cath trailed behind, laughing and sometimes breaking into a jog to catch up before lagging again.

Eden lunged forward to hurry and meet them but stopped herself. *I don't want to look too eager. I better wait.* She stood there another few seconds tapping her foot; then, one of them waved.

"Hey, Eden, we're glad you made it." It was Cath. *That lady is nice to everybody.* Eden took a deep breath, decided it would be rude to delay any longer, and ran toward them smiling. "Morning."

Cath was breathing hard. "You look adorable! Do you sleep with your makeup on?"

Marlene pumped her arms as she walked. "Cath, don't you know better than to ask a woman that?" Shaking her head at Cath's bare face and unkempt hair, she shrugged. "Well, maybe you don't. Hurry up, Eden. Kimberly thinks she's our drill sergeant. Maybe you can soften her up."

Kimberly increased her pace. "Not likely. We are only walking, ladies. Two more weeks of this, and you'll be able to jog the last two laps. Let's get going."

Eden fell in beside Kimberly and found their gait exhilarating but not exhausting. She watched Cath out of the corner of her eye, working hard to keep up but sporting a huge smile while doing it. Sprinting as best she could, Cath pulled up next to Eden and huffed out breathlessly, "So Eden, how long . . . have you been . . . in the ward?"

"Well, I've lived in the ward for the last three years, but we've only lived in our house for about seven months. Before then we lived in the apartments on Main Street."

Marlene hurried up beside them, so they were four abreast. "How did you ever get that house?" Marlene flipped her wrist to peek at her watch. "It wasn't even on the market."

Eden looked to Kimberly. "Are we done warming up?"

Kimberly took the hint and picked up the pace, but Marlene was undeterred. "I heard your place was supposed to be torn down and made into a park for the development."

Eden took a deep breath and pushed herself a little faster. She had heard those identical words from Mrs. Murdock and other disgruntled neighbors at least a hundred times. *I suppose I could simply print out a flyer with my response and put it on all their doors, so the whole neighborhood would leave me alone,* she thought. The great irony was that finding her house had seemed like such a miracle. Maybe, just maybe, these women would understand, being members of the Church.

"Well, we'd been looking for a place for months but couldn't find anything we could afford in the area. Then our realtor called. Apparently, she'd been talking to the developer that afternoon, and he said his wife wanted it to go to a young family." Eden slowed a bit and turned to the other sisters. "Immediately, she thought of us. The price was a little more than we had planned, but by some miracle we squeezed into it. It's a great investment, and we plan on fixing it up over time."

Marlene moved in closer and raised her eyebrows. "How much time?"

Eden looked over her shoulder at the house. It did look shabby, but siding cost over $30,000 and, because there were lead paint issues, even to have it professionally painted was almost $20,000. She knew it could be years before they could afford to do much of anything. "Soon. Josh has been working a lot of overtime and with the baby—well, you know how it is—but it will be wonderful when we get it all done."

Cath smiled. "I bet it will."

Marlene shook her head in disgust. "The problem is not a matter of *if*—it's a matter of *when*. Are we talking anytime before the Millennium?"

"You're a hoot!" Cath laughed. "Now, Eden, is there anything we can help you with in the meantime? We are your visiting teachers, after all. Do you need meals brought in, household chores you'd like help with?"

"Yeah," Marlene muttered out the side of her mouth, "and maybe we could even get you an ugly refrigerator magnet with a saying on it."

Cath giggled. "Or better yet, write it out on your driveway with sidewalk chalk. But seriously." She touched Eden's arm and looked in her eyes as they slowed. "I could bring my boys over and help with that yard."

Eden softened and wondered if she could really ask for the much-needed help. Then Marlene interrupted, "Anything, that is, except babysitting. I'm out of the baby business. After five kids, I've paid my dues. They tried to call me into the nursery when we first got here, and

I told the bishop straight out that he was crazy. I love to visit the grand-kids, but after three days I need my space." Marlene moved up next to Kimberly. "I mean, you have the right idea, waiting to have kids. I wish I had been that smart."

"Let's pick up the pace, ladies." Kimberly moved away from Mar-lene and positioned herself beside Eden, speaking to her for the first time. "So, Eden, what did you do before you had kids? What's your degree in?"

Eden clenched her jaw and increased her stride. "I was going to school at BYU–I to become a nurse when I met Josh. He was a senior, so I had a choice to make, and I chose to have a family instead of a career." Eden watched as Kimberly's gaze dropped to the ground. The look on her face mirrored how Eden had felt all week. The gloom of her impending problems with the state family services began to hedge in and fill her mind with a dark cloud.

Kimberly tightened her lips and passed Eden, who, in that moment, determined that she would not fall behind. The two older women were left in the dust, as they each competed in the unspoken challenge. Eden and Kimberly raced neck and neck around the cul-de-sac, until Eden found herself fascinated by something she had never seen before and suddenly stopped. The gateway at the end of the road was open.

Eden had never seen anyone go in or out, and after a while had stopped thinking about it. But now the massive gates were swung wide open, and she could see a good-sized shed or old garage surrounded with heavy growth halfway up the scraggly gravel driveway that she hadn't even known was there.

A burnt foundation of a large building stood next to it with a thick black skeleton of scorched beams that were slowly being swallowed up by vines and with underbrush squeezing through and creeping up each surface. An old car was parked there, and in the dim of the morning, it looked like the lights were on in the garage.

"Hey, do you think someone is living there?" Cath called from behind, voicing what they were all thinking. Eden, Kimberly, and Marlene stood side by side, staring on curiously.

"Could be," said Kimberly after a moment. Then, looking specifi-cally in Marlene's direction, she added, "But I'm sure it's none of our business."

Totally oblivious, Marlene took three or four steps up the driveway and put her hands on her hips. "That is the Lewis mansion. It burned down thirty years ago. Isn't it remarkable?" She returned to the group with her nose in the air. "As an officer in the homeowners' association, we do not want squatters ruining that historic landmark. I'll report it to Helen as soon as we get home."

Eden wondered why Marlene didn't consider her home a landmark too. It was the original homestead built before the prohibition started, when the Lewises apparently made all their money, but she kept her mouth shut and started following Kimberly again.

Still, her mind wouldn't let go of the idea of Marlene and Helen Murdock, the homeowners' president, talking, and she wondered how many conversations they had with her at the center.

As the group headed back past her house in awkward silence, Eden saw Hayden crying at the front window. From the condensation on the bathroom window, she guessed that Josh was in the shower and looked back to see Marlene gawking at her son. "Someone certainly is unhappy."

Eden began to worry about what the others would think. She felt guilty that she was stealing Hayden's and Josh's time. The pit in her stomach came back about all that had happened on Sunday and what it would mean in the future. The policemen had said a caseworker would be coming in the next few weeks, and Eden might have to ask these women for references. She couldn't offend them, but how could she let her little boy cry unchecked? She struggled with what to do.

Halfway down the road, Eden couldn't stand it anymore and turned to the others. "I sort of have a cramp in my side. I think this is enough for today. I'll probably do better tomorrow. Sorry. Thanks."

Cath paused and let out a heavy sigh. "That's fine, Eden. It was so nice to get to know you better. We'll catch you tomorrow, bright and early."

"Bye," Eden said as she dashed back home at full speed to comfort her little boy and get breakfast for her husband.

Kimberly turned to Marlene after watching her leave. "I'll say one thing for sure—that girl does not have a cramp."

· · · · ·

Marlene surreptitiously dabbed her forehead with a fresh Kleenex from her right pocket; her left was bulging with the eight slightly used tissues she planned on disposing of as soon as she completed her last goal of the morning. She had watched to make certain Kimberly had closed her door and Cath was headed home. She looked over her shoulder once more at the blue monstrosity behind her before heading up the walk and rapping lightly on the door that opened almost immediately.

"Marlene, what a nice surprise." Helen gave a conservative grin and stood at the door with no indication of inviting her in.

"I wanted you to know that I think someone is living in the old garage at the end of the street. I saw—"

"Isa Lewis moved in yesterday. Her husband was the man who promised us the park." She scowled and put a hand to her chest. "I thought we had the place condemned, but he put it up for sale before we could finish the paperwork."

"You condemned the garage?"

"No, no." Helen waved her hand. "The house across the street. We even had a city ordinance passed that if properties aren't brought up to code in six months, individual citizens could foot the bill for immediate demolition. All that work for nothing."

"What?" Marlene eyes were glassing over. "Are you talking about Eden's house?"

"So you've met her?" Helen opened the door wider.

"Yes. We've begun walking together." Marlene dabbed her forehead again and ran a hand across her hair, making sure it was in place.

"Perfect. I couldn't have planned it better myself. In the next day or so, I would be most grateful if you would remind her of our offer to purchase her property."

"Her property?"

"She'll know what you're talking about, trust me." Helen gave Marlene her largest smile, which looked like it didn't quite fit on her bare lips. "Now, you came about Isa, right?"

"Yes, the lady at the end of the street. Will she be here long?"

"We certainly hope so. You know, we are old childhood friends. Apparently, she has seen the light and is finally divorcing that liar of a husband. If she enjoys the neighborhood, word is that she might rebuild the mansion, increasing all of our home values in the process. So be nice to her."

"Yes, of course." Marlene stuttered.

"Now, thank you for your faithful service as a member of the homeowner's association council. I know I can always count on you." With that, Helen closed her door, leaving Marlene inches from the painted surface with her mouth still open.

"You're welcome," she said softly to herself and turned to walk home, craning her neck at regular intervals toward the end of the cul-de-sac. "Wow, a real mansion."

7

A Strange Intensity

On Thursday Miley woke up an hour early. Eden jumped out of bed, fed the baby, threw on her sweats, and then lay back down. It had been a hard week. As each day progressed, her anxiety increased. Every time the doorbell rang, she worried. Was it someone from family services? The stress was getting to her, but she didn't want to upset Josh with her feelings, so she didn't mention it. There was no way she was going to tell her mother. Carrying that burden alone was taking its toll, and she was exhausted. Eden dozed off.

Later she rolled over lazily and looked at the clock. Throwing off the covers, she dashed for the bathroom in a panic. She had slept in. Without even touching up her face, she ran a brush through her hair. Four minutes later at 6:03, Eden was outside, turning to lock the front door.

Suddenly a hand smacked down against her shoulder. "You up for a race?" Kimberly sprinted away down the front walk to the street.

"Sure." Eden was pleasantly surprised by Kimberly's impromptu familiarity. She gave chase, acting like she didn't have a care in the world. Soon the two were running flat out to the end of the cul-de-sac with Marlene and Cath far behind.

Eden couldn't believe how rested she felt for the first time all week and vowed she wouldn't let her mind fill with the dread that had tainted every thought since Sunday. She let herself enjoy the exertion of trying to catch up with Kimberly and was almost nose to nose when her friend came to an abrupt stop. Eden followed suit. They watched as an old faded blue Cadillac rumbled down the overgrown driveway at breakneck speed, screeching to a halt right in front of them.

A woman with a mop of messy hair, wearing a bright orange prison jumpsuit covered in dabs of paint, shoved her car door open and hurried over to close the gate behind her. Kimberly and Eden watched in astonishment and were soon joined by a pointing, giggling Marlene, who was obviously entertained by the strange woman.

It felt good to be silly, and Eden began laughing softly too at the odd lady. When Cath caught up to them, her face shone with delight, and she trotted forward without hesitation. "Hi, I don't think we've met. I'm Cath Reed, and these are my friends, Eden, Kimberly, and Marlene. Are you new to the neighborhood?"

The woman looked flustered. "What? Oh, no, I grew up here. I've lived here forever. I just ran out of red. Can you believe it? I'm totally out, and it's the most important color of all. Well, I've got to run while the inspiration is fresh. Nothing is worse than spoiled creativity, you know." Hopping in the car, the woman rolled down her window and shouted, "Come by and visit any time." She roared away in a cloud of dust.

Marlene looked at her friends and stuck out her tongue. "Have you ever seen such a loon in your entire life?"

Kimberly shook her head at Marlene's childishness and started walking away indignantly. "She may have her reasons."

Cath smiled. "Well, I liked her. She has a unique intensity that I admire. That's the sort of person who is probably a brilliant artist."

"Or a serial killer," Eden said to be funny but, on seeing Cath's expression, felt bad and added, "I mean, she seemed different."

"You are spot on," Marlene agreed, "but I don't think she's dangerous. In fact, I hear she's very wealthy and in the middle of a nasty divorce. If everything works out, Helen says she's going to rebuild that place and increase all of our home values." She covered her mouth. "Oh, and I forgot. I was supposed to be nice."

"Well, I'd say you failed on that front," Kimberly said under her breath.

Marlene continued unfazed. "Oh, and Cath, I totally know what you mean by that kind of intensity. I'm married to it. From sun up to sun down, Roy is outside working on the yard. He spent the last forty years as a farmer, and you'd think in our retirement he would find time for me, but instead he just tends the yard and the garden. Why, he even tends the neighbors' gardens. The other day he actually told me he was now a 'lawn artist.' Can you believe it?"

Cath shrugged. "I've seen your yard. The flowers are spilling out of the beds, and the grass looks like Astroturf. I'd say that's a pretty good description of what he does."

Marlene laughed to herself and then shook her head seriously. "No, thank you. I've had enough of that artsy-fartsy creative jazz. Perhaps she'll just stay to herself. I'll tell you, I don't need any more intensity in my life."

"I hear you," Eden chimed in.

Cath and Kimberly set off ahead. Eden started up again, and Marlene bent toward her and almost whispered, "By the way, have you had time to reconsider our offer?"

"What offer is that?"

"For the homeowners' association to buy your house."

Eden noticed the beige droplets around Marlene's brow where her foundation was melting and the small wrinkles around her eyes. "I can't believe you just asked me that."

Marlene flattened out her mouth and lifted an eyebrow. "If ever you change your mind, I'm here."

Marlene hurried forward while Eden lagged behind. *So most of my neighbors still want to get rid of us,* she thought. In a way she felt a kinship to the strange woman she had seen living apart from what other people considered normal. The sad truth was that all Eden wanted was to fit in.

Kimberly was halfway up the block, calling to the other three women to hurry up. Eden was ripped from her thoughts by the sight of her open front door. She watched Kimberly leave the road, and then run beside the house and back to the ditch with Cath in hot pursuit. Marlene stood at the street's edge, wringing her hands. "Kimberly thinks she saw your kid out again. They went after him."

Eden sprinted into the brush without hesitation. The other women were calling Hayden's name and wading through the waist-high weeds, filled with prickers and brambles. Eden could feel her shins being scratched but didn't care and tried to watch the grass for the slightest movement, hoping it would give away her son's position. She noticed a tuft of foxglove tremble unnaturally and dove forward to capture her son. Instead, a pheasant exploded into the air, squawking in surprise.

Eden rolled over and sat in the dirt, trying to calm her heart, which was jumping wildly in her chest. It was surprisingly peaceful on the ground surrounded by the slender stalks of grass. Eden lay hidden from the craziness of the rest of the world by the lush green leaves and thick foxtail heads above. Looking around, she noticed the bright blue and red of Hayden's Spiderman pajamas and then made out his grinning face hiding gleefully beside a stump just a few feet away. Eden shook her head and wondered what she could do to help him understand how not funny this was.

In that same moment she realized that it was as much her fault as his. She must not have completely bolted the door when she left. Sitting in the tall grass, Eden knew one thing for certain—she couldn't possibly do this anymore. No matter how much she wanted or needed this time to herself, it wasn't hers. That was the way it was. It was her lot in life, and she had to accept it.

When Hayden caught sight of his mom, he walked up and snuggled in her lap. She held him tight and stood wearily, calling to Kimberly and Cath, who were still searching and getting more frantic by the minute.

As they made their way over to Marlene, Kimberly looked furious. "I've got to go home." Kimberly's words were as clipped as her pace, and Eden watched her sprint away.

Cath calmly patted Eden on the back. "It's all right. This is only a phase he's going through. I once had to call the police to help find my youngest son. He was sleeping in the garage—overnight."

Marlene raised her chin. "Well, I never had that happen to me. I've always known exactly where my kids were, and furthermore, I think it is a mother's job to teach them to behave. My word, it is going to take me all morning to get over this. I can't believe it."

Cath shook her head at her friend's comment and turned to Eden with concern. "If you need anything, please call me—even if you only need a break for a few hours. This is my first year without preschoolers, and it would be a treat for me to watch them."

Eden shook her head. "I'm fine," she said, lowering her gaze. Cath's shins sported bright red crosshatches from the thorns beneath her knee-length biker shorts, and Eden hurried even faster through her front door, propelled by shame. Once she entered the living room, she could hear Miley's frantic sobs and wondered how long the baby had been crying.

Turning into her bedroom, she encountered the saddest surprise of all—her exhausted husband was still fast asleep with a pillow clamped over his head. His project at work was falling behind, and he had been putting in extra hours to bring it back on schedule. These early mornings were too much. Eden didn't disturb him but turned to take care of the baby while Hayden played happily with his toys. It was clear this wasn't working.

·　·　·　·　·

Marlene waited until Cath was far ahead before doubling back to Helen's house. Despite the early hour, Helen answered on the second knock, fully dressed, and this time invited Marlene in. "Did you talk to her?"

"Helen, she's not going to budge. I could see it in her eyes."

Helen's face pruned up as she paced back and forth in her empty hallway. "Then we'll simply have to escalate the issue."

"I've been thinking." Marlene lifted a finger. "Maybe we could all get together and help them paint so it doesn't look so bad."

Helen put her hand on the knob and opened the door. "You keep thinking about it, and we'll discuss the options at our next meeting." Without realizing it, Marlene found herself back on the front porch. "Good day to you."

·　·　·　·　·

Helen threw the door shut and ran to the phone. It rang four times before a sleepy voice came on the line. "It's Fran."

"Helen Murdock here. I need to get into the town hall immediately and check some files."

"Mrs. Murdock, this is my home number. The door opens at nine. Please don't call me again." The line went dead.

That lazy ninny. She punched in the numbers and waited another five rings. "Yes." The voice answered in the middle of a yawn.

"I don't think you understand. As the city secretary, it is your duty to let me check these files immediately."

"Mrs. Murdock? Look, you have a key. Let yourself in. I've got another half an hour to sleep, so leave me alone." Fran hung up again.

Murdock shook her head in frustration and hit redial. It picked up on the first ring, and she plowed right in without letting the city secretary get a word in edgewise. "You have the legal responsibility to watch over official government documents, and you're telling me you'd let just anyone go through them at will? That is hardly responsible."

"I don't consider you just anyone, Ms. Murdock." Fran answered. *"You are the biggest pain in the butt I've ever met,"* she said under her breath. Then, clearing her throat, Fran continued, "If this is so important to you, go on ahead and do what you want. I'll be there at nine."

Helen smiled as she hung up. "Well, I warned her."

The ample purse on Helen's shoulder didn't slow her down as she marched up the road at a brisk clip. She rounded the corner of the main highway and hurried over to the small City Hall that sat in an empty field less than a fourth of a mile from her home. Helen looked both ways before inserting the key in the lock and slid through the door, feeling a thrill at her indiscretion. She knew exactly where the file was and hoped it contained some ammunition that would be useful.

A fine dust lifted from the seldom-opened drawer, filling the room with the smell of an old schoolroom on the first day of autumn. Helen rifled through the brittle records until she found the one on the Lewis Estate. The folder was the thickest in the drawer, and she gently lifted it and laid it respectfully on the table. She took a deep breath and rubbed her hands together, getting up the courage to pull back the reddish brown cover and reveal the information inside. *I've been given permission. This is entirely legal,* she told herself again, lifting her chin proudly.

She reached out a liver-spotted hand and quickly flipped the page open. Her eyes were immediately drawn to the corner of a light blue sticky note that stuck out among the aged photographs, tax records, and platted blueprints. She pulled at it and extricated the official-looking memo. It took her a few minutes to fish her reading glasses out of her large shoulder bag and set them properly on her nose, but as she did, a wide grin seeped across her face.

"Good girl, Helen," she said, laughing to herself. Carefully, she placed the memo back on top of the folder, returned it to its place, and shut the drawer tight. "You deserve an A-plus."

8

Unexpected Visitors

Eden was haunted with an unsettled feeling for the rest of the morning. Would today's escape be reported? Could it make matters worse with the state? When, if ever, would they even show up? Would they really take away her children? Was she that bad of a mother?

The worry was like a deep abyss, and Eden teetered on the edge, ready to be consumed by it. She wanted to talk to someone, but who would understand? After seeing Kimberly's face and listening to Marlene's biting words, there was nobody she could trust to help her. Cath had offered but she had four children and would certainly be too busy. Poor Josh was doing his best. She couldn't ask anything more of him. Eden closed her eyes and tried to pray, but the words seemed just out of reach. The truth was, she didn't even know what to ask for. She felt completely alone and at last whispered, "Heavenly Father, just send someone."

After feeding the baby, Eden decided the only answer was to roll up her sleeves. She made a fabulous breakfast of sausage, eggs, toast, and orange juice for Josh, who gobbled down a few bites before running out the door half an hour late for work. Then she encouraged Hayden to help her with the dishes, which consisted of him sitting on the kitchen counter next to her and getting his feet wet in the warm soapy water while she did the actual washing.

He was fascinated by the bubbles, and they even made bubble beards, which got Hayden giggling like crazy. When they finished there was as much water on the floor as in the sink, but that was okay too. Eden mopped the floor and gave Hayden a rag to slosh around beside her. By the time she plopped him in the tub, her little boy looked like she had mopped the floor with him— every inch of his clothes was wet and covered with grime—but the kitchen floor looked great.

Once Hayden was dressed in fresh clothes, she laid him down, and he was out cold. The crazy morning had exhausted him. After carefully bolting the front door, Eden took a shower, did her hair and got her makeup all done up. When the baby woke up, Eden was ready to face the day and soon had Miley on her hip as she vacuumed the front room, tidied up the bedrooms, and started a load of laundry. Eden was feeling pretty pleased with her accomplishments by the time the doorbell rang, and suddenly the heavy cloud of dread returned to her mind.

"Hi, there." An elderly man holding a flat of various plants stood at the door with a huge smile on his face. "I'm Roy. I belong to Marlene. Now I know what you're thinkin'. I'm nothing more than a sow's ear, but I sure hope that don't make poor Marlene the sow."

He laughed aloud at his own joke with his mouth wide open like a braying mule, and Eden smiled in spite of herself. "Well, I'll tell you, princess, Marlene spilled the beans about your troubles this morning, but don't take it personally. Why, when our kids were little they got into all kinds of messes. One time Troy, my oldest—must have been about three—fell in the irrigation ditch and got sucked right through the pipe. Marlene didn't even notice. If I hadn't seen his little soaked up diaper floating like a marshmallow in hot chocolate down the other side of the open ditch and snatched him out when I did, I hate to think what would have happened.

"Another time, Susie and Greg were playing in the silo at harvest time and nearly got buried alive. Luckily, I heard 'em screaming just in the nick of time. And don't even get me started on the time I took the kids for a ride in the bucket of the front-loader, but I guess that one was my own fault. Anyway, what I'm saying is don't feel bad. All kids need a posse of guardian angels lookin' after 'em or none of us would have made it to adulthood."

Eden scratched her head, wondering if Marlene was a hypocrite or if she'd simply forgotten what it was really like. But Roy's infectious drawl brought her back to the present.

"Now, I brought over these little pretties to brighten up your day, but you don't need dessert, you need the whole meal. Why it looks like the back end of this big old Saint Bernard that used to live down the lane from us. You never saw such a tangled up mangy mess in your life."

Roy did a full circle, taking in the knee-high weed garden around him that was their front yard.

"I know it's awful but—" she began to apologize.

"Never you mind," he continued, not even noticing her distress. "I'll run down, get the tractor, and we'll get this place under control in no time. It'll be great."

Before she could protest, Roy trotted off like an old work horse, and Eden looked at Miley with a quizzical expression. "I would never have put those two together."

By eleven Roy was done. "This is incredible." Eden stared at the transformation. Not only had he edged and mowed the front lawn, but he'd bagged the clippings, started a compost heap, and planted the flowers he brought.

As Roy got ready to leave, he turned. "Remember to keep those babies in the flower bed moist." He pointed at the seedlings. "Now the back is going to take a little more doing, but I'd be mighty grateful if you'd let me work on those forty in a few."

Eden nodded. "That would be wonderful, but it's really just under an acre." Roy knowingly winked and trotted away.

With the front lawn trim and the sun shining, Eden encouraged Hayden to help her pull the Little Tykes toys off the porch and put them around the front yard. While Miley lay happily on a blanket in the grass, he scrambled up and down the slide like a mountain climber, never quite grasping the concept of actually sliding, hid in the plastic playhouse while Eden played peek-a-boo through the windows, and then jumped up on the rocking horse and began riding with forceful determination.

Eden watched his intensity as he thrashed back and forth, trying to make the light blue plastic pony go faster, and knew this trait would probably be one of Hayden's greatest gifts as a grown man. It was just a little challenging to deal with in a toddler.

The crunch of leaves behind her made Eden twirl around. There stood Helen Murdock in her gardening gloves and hat. One of the sisters in the ward had told her that Mrs. Murdock had been the meanest math teacher in high school. The kids had thrown a party for her when she retired out of gratitude that she was leaving. Word had it that she had invested well and, after years of penny pinching on a tight salary, had bought her dream house right across the street and retired. Now her full-time efforts were focused on being president of the homeowners' association and making Eden's life miserable.

"Mrs. Duncan," she began in her formal nasal tone, "I believe we have something to discuss. I have it on good authority that you plan on remodeling this hovel in the near future. Apparently, the plans to turn this lot into a park as promised to forty-seven percent of the current residents of Timberlake cannot be legally disputed because it was never issued in writing, but in the best interest of everyone around you, I plan on rectifying that error. I would like a written schedule of your planned renovations to be brought before the next meeting in order to safeguard our largest investments—our homes."

Eden smiled and tried her hardest to keep up appearances. She had hoped when she first met Mrs. Murdock that the woman would become a type of grandmother figure to her children. That dream had died long ago. Now she only hoped to get back in her house without both of her children witnessing a full blown attack.

Reaching back, she picked up her baby and tried to use the child as an excuse to put distance between them. Hayden was still going strong on the rocking horse, so a quick exit would be difficult. "Helen, with the new baby and everything else going on, life has been so busy. It may be a few more months before we even think about it in that amount of detail. I'm sure you can understand."

"Not in the least, and it's Mrs. Murdock to you." She folded her arms across her chest and tapped her foot, looking up to the sky as if to call down the powers of heaven. When she finally fixed her gaze back on Eden, her eyes had an evil squint to them that almost looked as though they would shoot laser beams at her. "Mrs. Duncan, do you understand that your actions don't simply affect you but every one of your neighbors? Do you even read the papers? We are in the middle of a housing crisis, and your irresponsible behavior is stealing money out of the pockets of each family on this block." Helen took a step closer, but Eden held her ground, not wanting to be too far away from Hayden.

"This eyesore is not only bringing down housing values but may even affect the ability of responsible homeowners to sell our homes at all when the time comes. The simple fact is that your personal freedom to swing your fist ends at the tip of my nose, and, Mrs. Duncan, you have been punching me right in the face every day since you moved in. I'm sick of it. Do you know what it's like to have to look at this wreck every morning? If poor Roy wasn't so easily manipulated, your lawn would still be a disgrace. I will not have it. Do you understand?"

Eden nodded in stunned silence, expecting her neighbor to start talking about her "permanent record" any minute.

Mrs. Murdock continued her tirade by adding sweeping hand gestures. "But we will not take this situation lying down. Currently, you are not part of the homeowners' association, but we have decided to graciously allow your family to join and even waive the monthly fee, if you will give us a proposed schedule of improvements. After it is approved by the board, we would also ask for a signed affidavit that you will comply with the schedule or be heavily fined. It is for your family's own good. Trust me. Time is growing short. Soon it will be out of my hands. You do not want to lose one of your greatest assets." She looked at Hayden and raised her eyebrows.

The veiled threat was not lost on Eden, and she reached down with her free arm and jostled the young boy up on her free hip while he whined and tried to wiggle free to return to his place on the rocking horse. "Thank you for your kind offer, Helen," Eden said as politely as she could while struggling to keep Hayden in her grasp and not drop the baby. "I'll discuss it with Josh tonight and get back with you." Without another word Eden turned, struggled to get through the door with both arms full, and bolted it.

From behind its solid protection she could hear Murdock shout, "The cost of inaction can be the greatest cost of all."

Once inside, Eden deposited Hayden on the sofa and went to get a cool drink of water in the kitchen. She was so flustered by the entire encounter, she couldn't stop shaking. Walking back into the front room, she saw Hayden already asleep on the faded green sofa and covered him with the baby quilt. She sat in the rocking chair and hugged Miley to her, not sure what to do. She wondered if it was worth upsetting Josh over the whole incident.

One of the reasons they had bought the house was that it was not part of the homeowners' association. But could Mrs. Murdock really have that much power? Eden thought again about what had happened on Sunday, and her stomach began to ache at the impending "action" that was to be taken against her. This had been a challenging time, and Mrs. Murdock calling the police over and over was doing very little to make matters better.

Eden thought of the woman's constant scowl and pursed dry lips. It was like every bit of kindness was totally dried up inside of her, and the shell that was left was hard and ugly. Eden rocked back and forth, feeling the emotions swirl inside of her—a mix of anger, guilt, embarrassment, indignation, and concern. Her thoughts were interrupted by the doorbell, and Eden jumped up, certain that it was Mrs. Murdock with something else to gripe about.

Leaping to her feet, Eden marched up to the door, ready to stand up for herself for the first time. She would not be walked over again. *This time I'll tell that shriveled up monster that my life is none of her business and to leave my family alone.* With the baby cradled in her left arm, Eden yanked open the door with her right to find a woman about her own age wearing jeans, a natural cotton shirt, and dark rimmed glasses, and holding a clipboard.

"Is this the residence of," the girl looked down at her clipboard officially and then looked up, "Joshua and Eden Duncan?"

"I'm Eden Duncan. How can I help you?" she answered, thinking the young woman was trying to sell educational books or something.

"My name is Lisa. I'm a caseworker for Family Protective Services and was wondering if you had a few minutes to speak with me." The tone of her voice made it clear this was not a request but an order. The young woman walked right in the front door and marched around, inspecting the spotless kitchen and tidy room with the sleeping toddler on the couch.

Eden felt a little violated but sat down compliantly on the sofa next to Hayden while Lisa took her place on the rocking chair. The social worker almost seemed disappointed by what she saw and pulled a pen from her back pocket. "I've had time to review your file and wanted to make sure I understood it completely. It says here that you are currently unemployed without a college education."

Eden had never thought of it that way but supposed it was technically correct and nodded her head slightly. "Well, I'm home with the kids."

The young woman continued, "And you have had three separate incidences of extreme parental neglect."

Eden shook her head. "Hayden here has barely learned to walk. I was shocked the first time he opened the front door and ran out. I was over there loading the dishwasher and thought he was in here playing with toys. It seemed only minutes before a neighbor brought him back. We got a chain for the door the next day, but soon he found out he could wedge himself through the crack in the door with the chain still on, so we installed a deadbolt. This morning I thought I had locked it and must have not completely done so, because he slipped out again. It's a learning curve, but we're working on it."

The caseworker took copious notes and lifted her nose. "Oh, you had another incident? That's not in my records."

Eden hugged the baby tighter and decided to be quiet. It seemed like she was just making things worse.

"Mrs. Duncan, it sounds like you are doing the best that you are capable of and literally have your hands full." She looked at the baby with disdain. "Although there is no obvious evidence to convince me that this case should remain open, for procedural reasons, may I ask for the names of two of your neighbors and one medical or childcare expert who has worked with your son. If their testimonies coordinate with what I have seen here, your file will be closed as long as there are no more incidents."

Relieved, Eden began thinking. After Roy's sweet visit that morning she happily gave Roy and Marlene's name and asked if Cath Reed around the corner was sufficient. "We would prefer someone on your street," the studious-looking caseworker replied. Reluctantly, she mentioned Kimberly but worried about what she would say after being so upset that morning.

When it came to a medical or childcare expert, Eden was at a loss. She had gotten most of Hayden's immunizations at the clinic in town. Every time she went in, it was a different nurse. Other than that, he had never been sick, and he wasn't quite ready for preschool. Since she had the baby, she had never even used a babysitter. At last she thought about nursery and got Hillary's name and number off the ward directory. As the caseworker pulled away, Eden wasn't at all sure this was over.

* * * * *

Helen stood in her front yard smiling. She'd recognized the state issued vehicle as soon as it drove up and was impressed by their promptness. Now the game was afoot. That little girl had been amply warned. In two weeks change was coming, and it was entirely up to her as to which way the curtain would fall. One phone call and a mere three thousand dollars was all it would take, but she would give her the time. No one could say Helen Murdock wasn't fair. Either way, Helen knew she had won.

9

Nobody's There

From the time she closed the door behind the caseworker, Eden began to seriously worry. She ran to the phone and called each of the women she had given as references, but none were home. She struggled with the idea of leaving messages, but how do you tell someone that you are under investigation with the state for being a terrible mother? She hung up.

She paced the floor and wracked her brain for what to do. Finally, Eden turned back to the phone and called her mother. Although she only lived a few hours away, Eden rarely spoke to her. From the time Eden joined the Church in high school, there had been a wedge between them, and when she abandoned her schooling to get married, it ended whatever feeling was left. There were still the obligatory phone calls on holidays, but they no longer shared their day-to-day lives.

Her mom never married Eden's father, a man her mom had only briefly dated the year after graduating from high school. Eden still wasn't sure of the whole story, but she did know that her mom had tried to make up for it by being successful. She was the top-selling agent at her real estate brokerage and lately was working harder than ever. The phone rang once before her mother answered with a chipper, "It's Hope Lane. I'm here for you."

The same phrase was at the bottom of all her mom's business cards, and Eden rolled her eyes. She always thought it a little ironic, knowing her mother was never there for anyone. "Mom, do you have a second? I need to talk to someone."

"Yes, I have three seconds to be exact. What is it?" Eden could hear the shuffling of papers in the background and knew by the sound of her voice that her mom was at her desk reviewing documents or checking the real estate section of the paper, comparing ads.

"Mom, things aren't going well. This woman across the street has it in for me and turned me into the state because Hayden keeps escaping."

As the words poured out, Eden could feel the beginning of tears and breathed deeply, trying to stay composed.

"Eden, I know exactly what you're going through; things aren't going well here either. So many people are putting their houses up for sale, but so few are actually selling that it's a madhouse. The Realtors who are used to doing nothing for their commissions are going down in flames. At least that part's satisfying."

"But, Mom, she won't be happy until I'm gone." Eden tried to pull her mother back to the point. "Her friend even told me they'd offer fair market value for our home, so they could turn it into a park."

"Really?" Her mom suddenly seemed interested. "You know we had to get that high interest loan for you because the house was an 'as is' deal. Selling now would give you plenty of money for something in better condition. I have at least seven possibilities. I'll even halve my normal commission." Eden could hear her mom rattling papers again, probably reaching for a graphic.

"Mom, it's our home." She shook her head in despair. It was like they were on different planets. "Don't worry about it. I can't talk to you. Thanks anyway—for being there." The words felt like cotton in her mouth, and suddenly all the lonely afternoons and weekends she'd spent growing up while her mom worked seemed to ache fresh in her mind.

Eden had to acknowledge that a part of the reason she wanted to be such a great mother was so that her kids would never have to experience a childhood like hers, and now she was failing at that too.

"Well, I've got to run," her mom said impatiently in the pause. "Say hi to Jacob for me." There was a click on the other line, and Eden knew her mom was gone.

"His name is Josh," she screamed into the empty receiver and slammed it down. As she turned around, there stood a stunned Hayden.

Eden crouched down so she was looking in his face and smiled. "Sorry about that, buddy. I promise to never do that to you when you grow up, okay? I will never treat you like you don't exist."

Hayden stared at her blankly and started picking his nose. The quiet of the house was deafening. If she didn't find someone to talk to, she was going to explode. Josh couldn't be reached at work, and there was no one she could think of to call—no one. Eden tried to shake it off, but the loneliness was suffocating her. "Let's go to the grocery store. Doesn't that sound fun?"

10

Shopping Around

As Eden clicked Hayden into the shopping cart restraint and stuck the baby carrier in the basket behind, she wondered how she would have any room for the things she needed to buy. With exactly $31.57 to last until Friday, she didn't have an option of getting that much. They were low on milk and could always use more diapers. She also wanted something fresh to go with dinner. Despite her awful morning, at least she felt good about staying within budget.

The grocery store was bright and nearly empty. She wandered up the greeting card aisle and pulled out a few funny cards just for laughs. There was one with a plumber bending over. When you opened it, it said, "Don't crack up." Eden grinned, put it back, and headed for the milk.

All the two percent was sold out except for one gallon way in the back. She had to open the door with one hand and reach as far as she could. Even then she could only touch it. At last she stuck her whole head in the shelf space. Successful, she lifted out her prize and suddenly noticed Marlene over by the eggs.

"Marlene," Eden spoke up across the refrigerated section. "I tried to call you. It was so nice of Roy . . ."

The older woman didn't look up and headed down the aisle behind her. Eden was perplexed. She had only been a few yards away. Certainly, she had spoken loud enough. Perhaps Marlene had hearing issues she didn't know about. Eden stared after Marlene thoroughly confused but was soon brought back to reality by Hayden pulling at her shirt.

"Out, out, out!" he shouted, yanking on the strap that confined him.

"No, Hayden," Eden said, trying to calm him down. She hurried over to the health aisle to get diaper rash medicine. Then she'd be ready to go.

Hayden's discontent seemed to be growing exponentially, and he tucked his legs under him, trying to stand up against the belt that held fast. Eden shook her head and touched his face gently. "Soon sweetie, I promise," she whispered in his ear. Grabbing the medicine, she moved forward to the checkout.

"Oh, Marlene . . ." Eden waved as the woman rushed toward her to put her cart back and head for the exit without so much as turning her direction. "There is no way that woman could even pretend she didn't see me. What is she thinking?" Eden said to herself as she stuck the pack of gum Hayden had grabbed across the checkout lane back in its box. Her hands began to shake as she thought of the ramifications of Marlene giving her a bad report. She had to talk to her.

Eden began bouncing on her heels and looked for an easy escape route. The old man and haggard woman behind her had a huge cart of groceries and didn't look like they were willing to budge. Besides, Marlene was already across the parking lot. Miley began to stir, and Hayden leaned over the side of the cart, trying to slide out of the belt any way he could.

Defeated, she waited in line and paid for her purchases, more determined than ever to try to reach Marlene as soon as she got home. Once out the door, she rushed to the parking lot and buckled a squirming Hayden in his car seat, still thinking about what she could say to Marlene. She closed the car door and went to put the cart back, holding Miley in her baby carrier with her other hand, when she heard someone yell.

"Oh, Eden, what a coincidence!"

She turned to see Hillary emerging from the store.

Hillary ran across the parking lot. "I can't believe it. I was just talking to Marlene about you. Did you see her after I did?"

"Yes, I probably did." Eden wondered if she should jump to the worst conclusion.

"You know, she was telling me about her last ward that had a little boy a lot like Hayden. He was so disruptive and immature that they decided he might not be ready for nursery. In the handbook it says that eighteen months of age is only a guideline. It might be better for everyone if Hayden didn't go to nursery for a while. What do you think?"

"Fine. He won't be there on Sunday." Eden plodded to the car, not listening to the rest of Hillary's prattle. She buckled in Miley's car seat, turned on the engine, and pulled away with Hillary still standing in the same place staring after her.

Eden's eyes misted, making the world seem softer and indistinct. She tried to convince herself not to jump to conclusions, but the raw sting of rejection seemed to creep into every thought. For whatever reason, Marlene didn't like her and maybe worse.

She turned right onto the main road and changed lanes to get on the freeway, but as she looked over her shoulder to check her blind spot, her stomach lurched into her throat. Hayden's car seat was empty.

Eden nearly hit a car doing a U-turn in the middle of the road. She pulled in the parking lot so fast that the front of the car scraped on the curb. She parked in the handicapped spot and threw open the car door, looking around wildly but finding no sign of her son anywhere.

Racing into the store, she asked the stunned checkout clerks if they had seen a small boy. They all looked at her like she was crazy. She ran up and down the aisles, and the more time ticked away, the more she began to worry about poor Miley still in the car outside, which was still running. Frantic, she decided to go get the baby before continuing her search, but as she rounded the last closed checkout stand to slip out the exit, she looked down to find Hayden happily sitting in front of the rack of candy by the register surrounded by ripped up paper and little clear molded pieces of plastic.

She reached down, lifted him up on her hip, and picked up the mess around him. He'd been opening tubes of lipstick and sucking on them, hoping they were candy. The pink and red cases seemed intact, and Eden hurried up to the closest cashier and handed her the mess, "Sorry, he opened these."

"Then you'll have to pay for them," said the girl with huge earrings and bad teeth from behind the counter. "The total comes to $45.12." Eden swallowed and dug in her purse to get her credit card. Her only success of the week, her budget, was officially blown.

11
One Thin Blue Line

Sandra's stomach growled with anticipation as she unwrapped her bacon, cheese, and fresh tomato sandwich on whole wheat. It was her favorite and would make up for the fact that she had intentionally skipped breakfast. She smiled, remembering the success of her plan and wondered how long she could keep it up. By pretending to sleep in the first half hour, she arrived at seminary with only fifteen minutes left, the last ten of which were spent in the bathroom with her friends Madi and Amanda so they could finish getting ready. This was her third time of only having to endure five minutes of spiritual torture and still getting credit for it.

Sandra looked across the crowded school cafeteria, hoping her friends would show up when she felt the table tremble and turned to see who had joined her.

"It's your fault he left." Cory's spiked hair and black clothes made his menacing stare appear even more intense.

"What?" Sandra was thoroughly confused. Last year she had dated his older brother, Zee, for a few months. It had ended poorly, and she'd heard he'd run away over the summer, but she doubted it had anything to do with her. "You don't know what you're talking about."

"He left because you made him feel like dirt—you and your stuck-up perfect little family."

His harsh whisper annoyed her. "I know my family has issues, but stuck up? Come on." She tilted her head and stared at Zee's little brother. "Wait. Where is this coming from?" Cory was a freshman and

52

had been around all year, but he'd never spoken to her before. "Why are you bringing it up now?"

As her friends arrived, Cory got up and walked around the table until he was right behind her. "This isn't over, Reed."

There was something in his eyes that made Sandra worry about him, and she grabbed his arm without thinking. "Wait, Cory, it's not like that."

He winced, and she looked down. With his sleeve bunched in her hand, she could see the edge of an angry bruise. "Where'd you get that?"

He yanked back his arm. "Don't change the subject."

"Cory, are you okay?" Sandra felt her stomach clenching and started to get up.

He stared at her, and she thought he softened for a moment before rushing off. Sandra followed him with her eyes as he rushed out the door, but her concern for him lingered. Zee had mentioned his dad's short temper. *Something's not right, I know it.*

"What's that about?" Madi nudged Amanda. "Did Cory ask you out?" They giggled.

"It's not funny." Sandra sat down, still staring at the empty door. After a few minutes she turned back to her friends and threw her sandwich down. "I'm not hungry."

About four hours later, Sandra catapulted off the bus ahead of the other students and ran full bore to her house. *Maybe Mom can figure it out. If something's wrong, she'll know what to do.* She threw open the door. "Mom, Mom," Sandra called frantically.

Cath emerged at the top of the stairs with folded towels in one hand and a toilet scrubber in the other. "I just got a call from the bishop and the Beckmans. Their plane just landed, and they're due to arrive in less than two hours. Can you start on the kitchen?"

Sandra opened her mouth, but her mom was gone. She threw down her book bag in the hall and slammed the front door shut behind her. "Fine, I won't tell you."

· · · · ·

Eden let the phone ring and ring, but no one answered. It was frustrating that she had rushed from the car to make the call. Marlene's garage door had been closed so it was impossible to tell if she was not home or simply ignoring her call. At last, Eden threw the receiver on the couch, unbuckled the fussy baby from her car seat, fed her, and put her down for a nap. Then she put on Hayden's favorite video, a silly Barney knock-off, and walked into the kitchen to put away the groceries.

With her elbows on the counter, Eden held her head in her hands and closed her eyes. She needed someone to talk to, or she'd lose her mind. She thought about calling her visiting teachers, but they were the stupid walking group, and she had already tried. No one was home. Then she remembered there was one person she'd overlooked.

Eden picked up the phone and dialed Cath, hoping she'd be there. *Maybe she'll know what's up with Marlene.*

It was answered on the third ring. "Yes. I'm on the other line. What do you need?" Sandra's voice sounded perturbed.

"Oh, it's Eden. Can I talk to your mom?"

"Fine." There was a clunk as the phone was set hard on a surface, and Eden could hear a loud shout. "MOM! GET THE PHONE!" At least three other people were talking in raised voices in the background.

A second later Cath got on the line. "Eden, how nice to hear your voice." She sounded winded.

"Do you have a minute?"

"Actually, I don't. I just got a call from some close friends who are due to arrive in . . . oh, my gosh, is it really 3:30? I've got to run."

"Don't worry. It's nothing important." Eden bit her lip and began to set down the phone when she heard Cath's voice again. "What?" she asked.

"Would you like to come over tonight? The bishop and his wife are coming." Cath's tone seemed insistent. "It'll be fun. You know, the more the merrier."

"I wouldn't want to impose." Eden scrunched up her face and closed her eyes.

"Are you kidding? It'll make it more of a party. Besides I have built-in babysitters. What do you say?"

Eden hesitated. "All right. Can I bring anything?"

"You can bring those two beautiful babies and an empty stomach.

Kevin was just saying how he wanted to get to know Josh better. See you at six, okay?"

Eden hung up the phone and collapsed on the sofa next to Hayden. *Were Cath and her husband talking about us behind our backs too?* Through the rest of the video, she wondered if she should call them back and cancel. It was obviously a mercy date, and the chances of the whole evening being disrupted by Hayden running off or Miley throwing a crying fit were better than half.

As soon as the show ended, Hayden ran for the door and began trying to open it. Eden could hear the baby stirring and decided if she didn't get out and do something, she really would lose her mind. With the baby buckled in the stroller, they trotted up to the end of the cul-de-sac together. Hayden kept up the pace but never really took off. He seemed to be making progress. The old gate was still open, but no car was there. They began heading back up the street and passed their house on the right and Murdock's on the left. She also wasn't home. Eden felt relieved.

Marlene's garage door was still closed, so Eden guessed they weren't home, but when she got to Kimberly's house, there was a car in the driveway. The expression on Kimberly's face the last time Eden saw her had been burnt in her memory. Maybe if Kimberly got to know Hayden better and understood that he was just a busy little boy that liked to run, she'd get over it and not be so angry. Eden stared at the oak door. *Maybe she's sitting at home feeling as lonely as me.*

She reached down, unbuckled the baby, and held her in the crux of her arm while ringing the doorbell. Eden strained her neck to peek in the curtained window. She'd never actually been in any of these houses and began to wonder if they were all the same inside. She tapped her foot. Hayden reached up and rang the bell three more times before she caught him and held him back.

As Eden put Miley back in the stroller, certain no one was home, the door opened a crack. Kimberly looked cross. "Oh it's you. What do you need?"

"I came by to visit," Eden said, catching Hayden before he jumped off the front porch.

"It's not a good time. I'll call you," Kimberly said with her face set as stone.

Eden wondered what was going on. *Maybe she's still mad, but I gave her name as a reference—I have to speak with her.* She looked into Kimberly's eyes which were focused somewhere off in the distance. Eden sighed. "Thank you. I'll expect your call later then." She turned and walked away, not looking back, afraid that if she did, Kimberly would see the tears forming at the corners of her eyes.

Hayden rushed ahead while Eden pushed the stroller back home. Eden couldn't remember a time in her life when she had felt so utterly disconnected from all of humanity. In her driveway, she started to unbuckle the baby. Hayden was only a few feet from her when, out of nowhere, he gave her an impish grin.

"Don't you dare," Eden warned, but if he was only considering it, her words spurred him on. He shot up the road toward the cul-de-sac.

At least I don't have to worry about traffic. Eden took the baby and walked behind him, not overly concerned until she remembered the open gate at the end of the road. Sure enough, he rushed up the gravel driveway. She picked up her pace, jostling the baby, who began to wail with every step.

"Hayden, come back. No." He laughed, and Eden couldn't believe they were playing this game again.

By the time she got up to the little garage, she couldn't see Hayden anywhere. Eden wasn't sure what to do. She tiptoed up to the open door, feeling a little like Goldilocks, and peeked inside. She was surprised how big the house was. It had a large kitchen and living area with a hall leading to three other smaller rooms.

The main area was mostly empty with a few packing boxes stacked in the corner. At the center sat one bright pink chair with a floor lamp beside it. Even though that was the only furniture, it seemed to fill the room. The lamp shade was made of brightly colored stained glass including azure, chartreuse, pumpkin, and the same fuchsia color as the chair, with little clear prisms dangling around the bottom like a fringe that bounced color and light against the otherwise bland walls. The glass prisms were tinkling against each other much louder than a breeze would warrant.

Eden hugged the fussy baby and called breathlessly, "Hayden, please come to Mom." Though she knew she was trespassing, she didn't know what else to do. Hearing a soft giggle down the hall clinched it, and she stepped inside.

Slowly, she made her way forward, turned to the right and gasped. The room was filled with paintings. They weren't what you would call beautiful, but they were fascinating. Eden looked at the first one portraying a large military tank in the middle of a war. The tracks were worn and dirty, and the belly of the tank had been dented by hit after hit. It looked so real until her eyes were drawn to the gleaming cannon that transformed into a tube of lipstick.

Then she walked over to the next one and couldn't help but smile. A wall made up of shiny lipstick tubes gleamed in the sun. Standing behind them, protected from danger, was the most beautiful woman she had ever seen. She looked peaceful and free.

Eden stared at the pictures, trying to understand their meaning. Even Miley seemed fascinated for a second. Three sounds pulled Eden from her trance: the baby started fussing, an unmistakable rustle sounded behind her, and the crunch of tires on a gravel driveway echoed through the window. The last of the three noises sent a chill down her spine.

Quickly, she reached behind her, grabbed Hayden's hand before he ran off again, and began hurrying down the hall. She was halfway through the front room when she came face to face with the strange woman she had met the other day.

The woman's thin arms were filled with grocery bags. She didn't even seem surprised but simply smiled and said, "Hello again. I was hoping you would come to visit. I've got lunch. Would you care to join me?"

Eden blushed. "No, I'm sorry. We, uh, I've got to go." As she struggled for words, Hayden pulled out of her grasp and was out the door. Eden shook her head and began to give chase but stopped herself and turned back for one second. "Your paintings are incredible."

The older woman beamed, and Eden dashed away, determined to catch Hayden before he hit the street.

•　　•　　•　　•　　•

Kimberly closed her door and stared at the white plastic stick in her hand. There was no question that the line was blue. She was pregnant.

The grief of her past miscarriages began to hedge in. What had made her think it would be different this time? The doctors had said they couldn't find anything wrong, but something had to be. She knew it deep inside herself. Still, she hadn't listened to that voice, instead hoping for the impossible, and now, holding the evidence of the road ahead, she knew. She knew this would end in hard ragged grief just like all the others, and she knew she couldn't face it again.

12
Trapped in a Maze

The lasagna was delicious, but it didn't make up for how awkward Eden felt sitting at the large dining room table surrounded by people she barely knew. She still couldn't get their names straight. Cath's husband was either Keith or Kevin. She was too embarrassed that she hadn't caught it the first time to ask. Then there were two women she had never seen before. One was the bishop's wife, and the other worked with her as a designer. Her husband was some sort of retired inspector or something. She'd never seen any of them at church and guessed they were all inactive.

Even Cath's two older boys looked so much the same, she couldn't tell them apart. They were both in that nondescript age between childhood and puberty. At least she remembered Cath's youngest boy was Mike. He had fallen in love with Hayden, insisting they both sit with phone books on their chairs. The older boys flanked them on either side, helping Hayden tuck his napkin under his chin, cutting his food for him, and refilling his half-full cup. Hayden loved the attention, and she had never seen him so well-behaved.

"I think he's all done," one of Cath's older boys said. "Could we take Hayden to play on our super-maze on the back porch? We made it especially for him. It took every sheet in the house!"

"And most of the chairs." Cath winked.

Eden nodded, and the boys shot out the French doors to a billowing fortress that encompassed the entire back porch. Little ties of red yarn and piles of books secured the sheets in place. Eden leaned over and stared at the fluttering convoluted tunnel that showed no signs of the four boys who were swallowed up inside.

"What a cool mom Cath is," Josh whispered in her ear. "My mother never would have let us do that."

"I can see her point. It'd create a lot of unnecessary laundry." Eden wondered if she could be that type of mother and looked toward Cath, who was dabbing her eyes with a napkin. Eden looked around the table and noticed that Cath wasn't the only one trying to keep her emotions in check. Sandra had huge tears streaming down her face, and the other woman was close to hysterical.

"So you're really moving?" Sandra sniffled. "What will you do with the house and Gwen's garden?"

"I'm hoping to find someone who will love it as much as we do," the designer said, reaching across the table to lay her hand on Sandra's.

"Who's Gwen?" Eden blurted out.

"She's the one who brought us all together." The corners of Cath's mouth lifted. "She was my visiting teaching companion."

"And Gwen was almost comatose at the time, huh, Pattie." The bishop's wife slapped the table and nudged the woman beside her.

"Leave it to Cath to find a way to visit teach with her anyway." Pattie glanced at Eden and became serious. "You see, Cath wrote Gwen notes with crayons, so when she did wake up, she knew someone loved her. That's how we all met."

"Pattie lives in Gwen's house now. She inherited it. Gwen loved to garden, and the backyard is magical." Sandra seemed lost in thought for a moment and then turned forcibly to Pattie. "You've got to find someone that won't mind if I come visit—often."

"We'll try our best." Pattie tried to smile through her tears.

"So when is this move taking place?" Cath's husband asked.

Pattie's husband was a small-boned man with every hair in place, wearing a freshly pressed dress shirt and slacks. From the stiff way he sat, Eden could imagine that he would have felt more comfortable wearing a tie, too. Ralph Beckman put his napkin neatly in his lap, before replying, "We've been given a two weeks to get our affairs in order before we must present ourselves to corporate headquarters."

"At least you'll be here for the Nerd Party," Josh offered.

"Nerd Party? Who came up with that?" the bishop asked and

looked at Cath's husband. "Kevin?"

"No, it was Cath and the rest of the activities committee that thought it up. Everyone comes dressed up like a nerd, and the biggest nerd wins." Kevin nodded in his wife's direction.

"Actually, it was Roy who thought of it." Cath put down her fork. "Have you met Marlene's husband?"

"Yes, he's amazing," Eden answered softly.

"Isn't he the one who mowed our lawn this morning? Yeah, I'm sure that's who you said." Josh tapped his finger against his temple and then shook his head. "Well, it looks great. You should see it."

"I can't wait until tomorrow at walking group when I do." Cath smiled while Eden took another bite of food and stared at her plate to avoid eye contact, knowing that she wouldn't be there.

Kevin leaned forward. "Well, as I was saying, about this Nerd Party coming up . . ."

"The best part is I don't have to go." Sandra interrupted. "It's adults only, which I think says a lot about the nerd population."

Ralph and the bishop hooted and gave each other high fives, while Kevin tried to continue. "That may be so, but I think you're looking at the biggest nerd because I have a secret weapon. There is a plaid leisure suit that I've had since Cath and I first met that is the bomb! I've got this competition in the bag."

"Not so fast." Pattie laughed. "Ralph still wears pocket protectors. I mean, look at him."

"That's nothing." Jerri, the bishop's wife, lifted her hands. "Kurt has a pair of yellow polyester pants that scare little children."

"Okay, so we all married nerds." Cath clapped her hands together. "What do you say if the nerds do the dishes, and we go play with the kids on the back porch?"

"Whatever you thay, thweetie." Cath's husband stuck his front teeth out and gave a goofy smile, tripping intentionally as he got up.

Not to be outdone, the bishop laughed and snorted three times and then wiped his nose loudly. "It 'snot' a problem."

The retired inspector leapt up and began stacking plates. "Josh, would you like to wash?"

"Sure, if you don't expect me to compete on the nerd front." Josh stood up, flexing his biceps.

"That's great. Real nerds don't have to act the part," the inspector said, flicking his gaze at Cath's husband and the bishop. Josh deflated a little and headed to the kitchen.

Eden joined the other women as they went out back and was soon on her hands and knees, crawling around inside the sheets. She could hear Hayden laughing but hadn't found him yet.

"He's over here," she heard little Mike call and made a right. Suddenly the sheet lifted and Sandra squeezed into the crowded space and sat down cross-legged in front of her. "I need your advice."

Eden hunched down on her legs and cocked her head. "What's wrong?" She could tell by Sandra's face it was serious.

"Today at school there was this boy who had a bruise on his arm. He said it was nothing, but it's a family in the ward who has had problems in the past."

"What are you saying?" Eden squinted her eyes, trying to understand.

"I think his dad hit him. Hard. Maybe with something. You should have seen it. Do I go talk to the bishop or call the police? I don't know." Sandra looked down and bit her lip.

"Are you sure? Did you talk to the boy about it?" Eden swallowed. "You could really destroy their family by making an accusation like that if you're wrong. You have to be sure."

"What does that mean?" Sandra shook her head. "How can you be sure of anything? I *think* it's true from what I know about his dad and their family, but how can you actually *know anything*?" She paused. "Thanks for nothing."

Before Eden could open her mouth, Sandra was gone. The sheet in front of her wagged back and forth in the breeze, and Eden lowered her head, wondering how much of her answer was a reflection of her own issues. Guilt began to edge across her mind as she was bowled over by her excited toddler. "Mama!" He threw his arms around her, and Mike followed closely behind, laughing.

About half an hour later, the baby woke up and became fussy. Eden thanked Cath while Josh loaded the kids in the car. "Where's Sandra?" she asked, wanting to see her one more time.

Cath shook her head. "She went to bed early. You know, she hasn't been herself all day. I don't think she's feeling well."

Eden looked toward the stairs and swallowed. "Can you tell her I missed her?"

"Sure, but . . ." Cath put her hand on Eden's arm. "Are you all right?" Cath stared into her eyes frankly, but the sincere concern made Eden worried that she might actually see the truth.

"I'm fine. Thanks for the dinner." She rushed out of the house without looking back.

13
Strange Things Coming Up

The next morning, Eden didn't even try to wake up early. She wondered whether Kimberly, Cath, and Marlene were out power walking while she scrambled eggs for Josh and did a load of laundry. The day passed quickly, perhaps because Hayden slept most of the afternoon and into the evening. By the time Josh came home at seven thirty, her little boy was still fast asleep, and Miley was also taking a nap. Eden could hardly believe it. She sat alone at the table across from Josh, stunned at the unexpected break.

Right away Josh started telling her about his day. "You should have seen Cal's face when he realized he had entered the order wrong. He wanted so badly to blame me, but he couldn't, so he scrunched up his mouth and made his eyes bulge like this."

"You look like a monkey." Eden laughed.

"Exactly. It was all I could do not to start pounding my chest and making gorilla calls back at him, but that would have gotten me fired for sure."

"So, what are you going to do?"

"We can use all the transistors we produced, which leaves us three weeks ahead of schedule, but we still need two thousand more microprocessors by the end of next week. It's going to get hairy—that's all I can say—hairy." Then he cocked his head. "Like a gorilla." Josh pounded his chest and started howling and grunting like an ape.

Eden quieted him. "Shhh, you'll wake up the children."

"Sorry." Josh bowed his head. "And not just for that—I'll have to

64

work most of Saturday on the line."

"No, it's fine," Eden said, trying to smile. He had promised her that the long hours would be over this week. Now it looked like it would be another two weeks before anything would change.

She stabbed at her green beans and thought about how her mother used to call her to say she'd be home in ten minutes. After being alone all day, Eden would watch the clock, so looking forward to seeing her mom. Invariably, the time would come and go, and her mom still wouldn't be home. Every minute seemed to crawl, making the hours even more stark and empty. Finally, she'd learned to never believe her mom when she said ten minutes. She stopped looking at the clock and soon stopped looking forward to seeing her at all. Eden glanced at her husband, hoping the same thing would never happen to them.

"Are you okay?" Josh touched her hand.

"Why wouldn't I be?" Eden yanked it back and dropped her fork. "What could possibly be wrong?" She took a deep breath. "The women I gave as references to child protective services all went walking this morning, and I stood them up and didn't even call them."

"Well, you've had a hard day."

"The fact is, I didn't. Hayden slept most of the time, and Miley was an angel." She pushed her chair away from the table. "I just didn't want to think about it. I wanted life to be normal. Why us? Why do we have to deal with this? I'm trying my best to be a good parent, and now I have to prove it? It's too much, Josh."

"It'll be fine. You're doing a great job as a mom, Eden. You really are." The tenderness in his voice felt like a knife. She stood up and threw her napkin on the table.

"No, I'm not." She picked up her plate and walked it over to the sink. "I only wish I knew what I was doing wrong. I wish I knew how to teach Hayden better. I never had any little brothers or sisters. I didn't even really have a family. I don't know how to do this." She dropped her plate in the sink with a clank and covered her face with her hands.

Josh went to her and rested his hands gently on her shoulders. "I don't think anyone knows exactly how to do it; every kid is different. And by the time you do figure it out, you're a grandma; your kids are grown, and no one listens to you anyway."

She clamped her arms around his neck and pulled herself close to him. "Josh, I miss you. I feel so alone."

"I'm right here." He hugged her once and lowered his arms to return to his dinner, but Eden held on tight. After a few minutes, he said awkwardly, "Do you want to call my mom and see what she thinks about it? Would that help?"

She shoved him away. "What are you thinking? You can't tell your mother. This is only a stage he's going through. She thought I was too young to marry you in the first place. Please don't tell her about this, Josh, please."

He was amazed at her vehemence. "I'm sorry." Smoothing her hair, he pulled her close to his chest. "I promise I won't say a word. Don't worry, Eden. You're doing fine. It's all right. I promise."

She traced his handsome features with her eyes, and he slid his hand under her chin, lifting her lips to his. Eden closed her eyes, grateful for the warmth of his nearness. She had just let it begin to melt away her frustration when Hayden's cry pulled her back to reality.

"Maw, maw, no, maw!" Hayden stood up on the sofa with his arms outstretched.

Josh was the first one there and scooped him up. "Hey, bud, it's okay."

Hayden continued to scream and reach for his mom. Eden took him and immediately began to worry. "I think he's warm. I think he has a fever. I shouldn't have let him sleep so long."

"Let me see." Josh stepped forward as Hayden turned to him and vomited all over the front of his shirt. "Whoa, baby! If you didn't like the shirt, you could have told me."

With his stomach feeling better, Hayden snuggled up to his mom, and Josh went to take a shower.

14

Almost Missing It

J osh left for work before sunup the next morning while Eden was run ragged trying to keep the children apart, so Miley wouldn't get sick. Most of the day either Hayden was crying for her while she fed and changed the baby, or the baby was crying for her while she rocked a feverish Hayden.

On Sunday morning husband and wife lay in bed exhausted. Josh had gotten home about two in the morning after telling Cal there was no way he was working on Sunday. The entire line was grateful because without him, they let everyone have some much needed rest with a promise that they would return first thing on Monday. Both the children had finally fallen asleep a little after that.

Eden rolled over and looked at the clock. "Church starts in twenty minutes."

"I think Heavenly Father will understand if we miss it today. We've both been up most of the night."

"Maybe he will, but I wish . . ." She bit her lip.

Josh put an arm around her slim waist. "What do you wish? I'd love to grant your heart's desire. Name it, and it's yours."

"I sort of wish I could go. I think I need it. Besides, I still have to talk to Hillary, Kimberly, and Marlene about you know what." Eden swallowed back a wave of hopelessness and sighed.

"If you hop up right now, you could make it." His eyes brightened.

"No, you're too tired, and the baby won't last."

Josh sat up and laid a hand on her arm. "We'll be fine. I'll give her a bottle. Even if she doesn't take it well, she'll only cry half an hour tops. Look, if I can handle Cal ranting and raving for ten hours straight yesterday, a half an hour of an upset baby will be cake."

"Really?" Eden threw back the covers and leapt from bed.

"Sure, but you better get going while the gettin's good."

Eden rushed to the closet and grabbed the cute jumper that she had bought just before she'd found out she was expecting. It still had the tags on. She pulled it overhead, wearing a white t-shirt underneath and hurried for the bathroom.

As she walked, she could tell the jumper wasn't as great a fit as she had hoped. The skirt pulled a little, and it wasn't a really good cut, but it would have to do. With only minutes left, she brushed her teeth, ran a comb through her hair, and washed her face. After a light pass of her mascara wand and a little blush, Eden ran out the door.

As she drove into the parking lot, the clock read 8:52. She was amazed that she had gotten ready so quickly. Turning off the ignition, Eden flipped down the sun visor and took one last look in its little hidden mirror. *My mom would be horrified if she could see me now.* She pinched at her pale cheeks. *But I'm not here for her; I'm here for me.*

She slapped the mirror shut and jumped out of the car, almost skipping up the steps to church. This was a first. Since Hayden was born, she had never come to sacrament without children. Eden smiled as she envisioned being able to sit and actually ponder during the sacrament instead of wrestling with a toddler or sitting in the foyer or nursing mother's lounge. She was within ten yards of the front door when she heard her name and turned around to see who was calling.

"Eden!" Heather Gunnell, the Primary president, rushed up the stairs with her family. "Hi, life has been so busy. Yesterday was our quarterly Primary activity. It turned out great. How have you been doing? How's the baby?"

"Fine," Eden mumbled.

"You look so tired," Heather said with concern and then turned to continue through the door.

Putting a hand to her face, Eden immediately regretted not getting ready properly. As she pinched her cheeks again and smoothed her hair, she heard a sound coming from the front foyer. "Sister Gunnell is always an eight," TeeAnn stated loudly as her friends giggled.

Eden could see Hillary's daughter, TeeAnn, sitting in the middle of the sofa in the foyer with that outspoken twin Winnette on her right and another girl she didn't recognize to her left.

Heather's teenage daughter walked in. "Six. She's gotta lay off the Cheetos, if you know what I mean." Winnette's voice carried across the room.

Eden couldn't believe her ears. Those little imps were judging people as they walked through the door. She wondered if she could run to the back entrance of the church, but there were already two families behind her. There was no way around it. The throng was pushing her closer. She cringed and hurried through the foyer and into the chapel. As she passed she couldn't help but hear, "Wow, I can't believe how she's let herself go. Two."

In the chapel Eden sat in the far back corner against the wall, embarrassed to be seen. *I knew this jumper was too tight.* There were still a few minutes to go before the meeting began, and her eyes followed each family as they continued to arrive. Cath and her posse sat on the second row as always without noticing her. She could see the backs of the heads of her guests and the kids all engaged in cozy whispered conversations.

Around the room most people were busy greeting each other. A few stressed out individuals darted around searching for specific members to hand out assignments, trying to make use of that last little breath of time.

As she watched, Eden realized that she wasn't part of it— any of it. No one even looked her direction, and she wondered what she was doing wrong. She closed her eyes. *I come every week. I served in Primary for two years. I try to do what is right. What's wrong with me? Why don't I have a single friend?*

Eden sat alone, missing Josh and her babies. Right before the meeting began, Roy and Marlene rushed through the door and sat across the aisle from her. Roy gave her a happy wave, but Marlene seemed to be consciously avoiding eye contact. Eden wondered how she was going to tell her about using her as a reference.

As the meeting progressed, Eden strained her neck and glanced around the room over and over. It looked like Kimberly wasn't even there. Scanning every row three or four times, Eden realized Hillary wasn't there either. Then she remembered Hillary's daughters in the foyer. *No, Hillary's probably just hiding in the nursery.* Eden vowed to herself that as soon as she talked to Marlene and Hillary, she'd go straight home. She was relieved by the decision.

Right before the closing song, Eden snuck out of her seat and headed out to the hall. She pushed at the first door to the left, and it immediately hit a table, barring her way. A shrill voice called out, "It's not time yet. I have five more minutes!"

Eden tried to stick her head through the crack. "It's me. I've got to talk to you."

"Do you have Hayden with you?" the voice spat.

"No." Eden swallowed back her anger.

The door opened slowly to show Hillary's face wearing a smile not unlike that of a used car salesman. "Oh, Eden, I'm sorry. Some parents are so anxious for free day care that they drop their stinkers off the first second they can. I'm so glad we see eye to eye about Hayden. He wasn't ready."

"Actually, that's not what I wanted to talk to you about." Eden tried to keep her voice calm and even. "Now, this is confidential, but we're being investigated by the state." The words came out in a single stream, and Eden took a deep breath before going on.

"For child abuse?" Hillary's eyes got big.

"No!" Eden couldn't believe Hillary could think such a thing. "It's all a misunderstanding. Hayden has snuck out of the house a few times just like he does here at nursery. I've got this neighbor who constantly calls the police about him, and, well, I've given them your name as a reference. Someone will be calling you, and all I ask is that you be . . . kind."

Hillary lifted her chin. "I'll tell them the truth."

The sound of the door knocking against the table ended their conversation as three small toddlers bolted through the threshold. "Thank you, Hillary. Have a good day."

In the crowded hall, Eden hesitated about what to do next. The lack of sleep was getting to her, and she almost lost heart and headed for the door, but in the mill of people, she could see Marlene's teased and recently dyed hair, the color of orange juice, shining ahead. Eden dodged past two old men and tapped Marlene's shoulder as she opened the cultural hall doors. "Marlene, can we talk for a moment before class?"

Marlene looked skeptical but then shrugged and followed Eden further up the hall where it was less crowded. "What is this all about?" she asked innocently.

"I have a problem." Eden searched for the words but was interrupted.

"I have a problem too." Marlene folded her arms. "Why did you kill walking group?"

Eden looked at the anger in her eyes and stood there speechless as she saw Hillary racing down the hall.

"Eden, I'm so glad I found you." She hurried forward. "I've been thinking about what you said about being investigated by the state for not taking care of Hayden properly, and I was wondering what I could possibly say to them. I mean, I only see him at nursery. I don't know anything else about you guys. Will they investigate my family too to make sure I'm an appropriate witness? I think you better tell them I can't do it."

Marlene's eyebrows were raised so high, they almost got lost in her hairline, "The state really called you? I can't believe she did it."

Eden ignored the remark and turned to Hillary. "They only want to ask you a few questions about how he is around other children when he's here. That's all they should ask you. It's not a big deal, but I really need your help."

"What if they take him away from you? Will I be responsible? Will I have to watch him?"

"No one is going to take him away. They're going to ask you a few questions, that's all—I promise," Eden reassured her, feeling sick to her stomach at the prospect.

"Well, okay, if you're sure. I better get back to the kids." Hillary dashed back up the hall.

Eden turned to Marlene. "So you've probably guessed that's what I wanted to talk to you about. Please don't tell anyone. I put you down as a reference, if that's all right."

Marlene smiled and patted Eden on the arm, making her garish bracelets jingle. "Oh, sweetie, it will be fine. Don't you worry. I'll tell them all the nicest things about you."

"Thank you," Eden said, hardly believing it. She'd never heard Marlene say anything nice about anyone.

"Now I better be off. Roy will be holding a chair for me." Marlene bounced away seemingly anxious to join the class. Eden guessed it was because she planned on telling anyone who would listen about her new juicy piece of gossip.

Ready to go home, she was turning to head out the back door, when she heard a sound. "*Psst!*"

She looked around and then heard it again. "*Psssst!*"

The mother's lounge door was open a crack, and Eden had a good idea who was inside. When she opened the door, there was Sandra sitting on the counter. Eden smiled, relieved that someone cared she was there.

Sandra folded her arms and stared, her eyes nothing more than tight slits. "You lied."

Eden froze. "What?"

"I thought about it all night." Sandra swung her feet to the ground and got up. "You can't know anything. It's impossible to really know." She shook her head and sat down again.

Eden wanted to escape, but knew she couldn't. Leaning her back against the door, she lowered her head. "Is this about that boy?"

"I mean, how can you know anything unless you see it firsthand? I'd have to be there when his dad hit him, and if I waited for that to happen, he could be dead."

"But what if he just had an accident or something?" Eden whispered, not wanting to fight, but unwilling to give in.

"I don't know. What if he didn't? You're supposed to be the grown-up here. Tell me what to do."

"I can't. I don't know anything either." Eden put her hand on the doorknob behind her. "Why don't you ask your perfect mother?" Before Sandra could say another word, Eden bolted from the room into the empty hall, leaving the teenager with her mouth open.

Eden got a drink at the fountain, surprised by the anger she felt at both Cath and her daughter. She marched toward the back door thinking that at least Josh would be happy to see her if she got home early. But before she took two steps, a hand caught her arm. It was Brenda

Ramsey, the Relief Society president.

"Eden, I'm so glad I ran into you. You've been on my mind so much lately. How are things?"

Eden swallowed, knowing that within the hour Brenda would hear about her situation, but she wasn't quite willing to bring it up yet. "Fine," she said flatly.

"I hear you've started walking with Cath and her group. That's a pretty great bunch of women."

"Actually, I would be grateful if I could be put in a new visiting teaching assignment. I don't think it's working out." Eden wanted to add that they all hated her, but that wouldn't be entirely accurate. With Cath it was the other way around.

Brenda stared at her for a moment. She clasped Eden's hand and said, "Endure it just a little bit longer. You know, the best way to make connections with others is to serve them. Too many women worry about how little attention they're getting when instead they should be worried about how much they're giving. They worry about feeling lonely instead of looking around the room and wondering who else is feeling lonely that they can lift and love. You have so much to offer, Eden. Share it more. People need you. The Lord needs you."

Brenda walked away, and Eden stared after her, thinking she was daft. *I've got nothing to give. After taking care of the kids, there's nothing left. Financially, we're barely eking by. What could I possibly give anybody?* She marched out to her car and sped away.

15

The Blueberry House

renda's words continued to plague Eden all the way home. She had nothing to give. She was running on empty. There was nothing left. She wondered why she even went to church when all it did was make life harder. The last few weeks, she had left every Sunday wishing she hadn't gone. Wasn't church supposed to make you feel better?

She parked in front of her house and stared at the large front open window. Through it she could see Hayden and Josh wrestling in the front room. Her son's peals of laughter danced softly through the air like music. She strained to listen but couldn't hear the baby crying. Eden knew she should hurry inside to help, but somehow she didn't want to. She still felt so empty, like a sponge that had been wrung out even after it was totally dry.

Opening the car door, she put her feet on the pavement and sat there looking out into space. At last she stood and began walking up the street to get away from it all—away from the peeling paint and Mrs. Murdock and Kimberly and Marlene and all the other nameless staring eyes telling her she wasn't good enough. She passed the trees and thick groundcover that led to the wrought-iron fence and then stared at the open gate.

The strange woman's face came back, haunting her mind. She thought about the woman's odd reaction to finding her in the house with Hayden. It was odd that she wasn't surprised and even invited them to lunch. Eden remembered the interesting painting she had seen and suddenly realized the beat-up tank was her. She was in a war and had taken so many hits that she was almost ready to give in. But why was the cannon a lipstick tube? It didn't make sense.

Suddenly, she felt the urge to talk to the woman about it but was worried. What if she was busy or didn't really want her to come like when she tried to visit Kimberly? But Eden knew she was making excuses. The woman had invited her to come back.

Strangely enough, it was the Relief Society president's words that tipped the scales. *Maybe this is a way I can be of service. I have nothing else to give, but I could give this woman a few minutes of my time.*

Eden had only made it halfway up the gravel driveway before the door flew open. Dressed in conservative sandals, a starched linen shirt, and with her hair brushed neatly into a tight bun, she hardly looked like the same person. "Welcome, welcome, I had hoped you'd come to visit. You're my new neighbor, aren't you? I can't tell you how pleased I am that you live in the blueberry house. I have such happy memories of it as a child. Come in! Come in!"

Eden smiled and followed her through the door. The boxes were gone, and the hot pink chair was now joined by a cream-colored hand with the palm open and fingers curled up big enough to sit in. An overgrown ficus tree took up a good portion of the room, and one large pink polka dot was painted in the center of the far wall. Eden sat in the hand chair, and the woman curled up in her pink throne.

"So tell me everything. What's your name? Your little boy is so cute and so is your baby. You're incredibly blessed. Do you know that?"

"Um, well, I'm Eden." She said dodging the question. "My boy's Hayden, and my baby is Miley. Sorry about the other day. You see, Hayden likes to run away."

"Don't we all? He's a man after my own heart. Haven't you ever wanted to run away?"

Eden blushed. That was sort of why she was here now. The woman gave a knowing smile and continued, "I'm Isa, and I bet you're wondering what I'm doing here." She leaned forward and whispered, "Well, I ran away too."

"You what?" Eden asked.

"I ran away, years ago. First, I ran from my husband because he couldn't understand me. Then, from my children who had grown up and didn't need me anymore. I ran away from my friends because they didn't get where I was coming from. You know, the problem with running away is that in the end, you find you've succeeded, and you're all alone."

The ticking of the kitchen clock became the loudest noise in the room. After a few moments Eden said, "I heard you're getting a divorce. I'm sorry."

"Don't be. Divorce is a death of something beautiful, but the sad truth is, our marriage died years ago. The worst part is that we both murdered it in a way. Still, the good thing coming out of all this is that I'm finally waking up—little by little anyway."

"I saw your paintings. Are those helping?"

"Yes, but the first few aren't really truthful. I thought they were, but now I know I was wrong."

"Really?" Eden dropped her jaw. "Because I totally got it. Some days I feel just like that tank, tired of taking hit after hit."

"Come with me." Isa stood up and took her hand. Together they walked down the dim hall to the room where the picture stood on an easel. "The tank is right. That's just how I felt when Charles told me we were through, like I'd barely made it through a horrible battle. But you know what's wrong, don't you?"

"I'm not sure."

She pointed to the lipstick cannon. "It's not a very effective weapon, is it?"

"What do you mean?"

"Oh, you know." Isa made a little circle with her hand trying to search for the right words. "Lipstick, makeup in general, represents that façade we put on for the world to see. We keep up appearances and cover up the things about us that are real but not very pretty. It may work for a little while, but in the end, it only pushes people away."

Eden looked at the other two pictures. "I like this one. The wall seems to keep the woman protected." Eden saw the beautiful woman behind the huge gleaming golden tubes placed side by side, keeping her safe.

"Well, that's what I first thought too. That's why I painted it, but then I realized they were keeping her alone. So I did the next one."

Eden walked up to the canvas and looked at it closely. It was a picture of a woman watering a garden of open lipstick tubes that had grown bright red thorns. The woman's face was empty and a little sad.

Eden wasn't sure what it meant but didn't like the picture. "I probably should go now." She cleared her throat.

The two women moved toward the front door, and Eden caught a glimpse of the scorched beams and winding staircase still partially standing through the window. "I bet the mansion was incredible when it was here. Did you ever see it?

"Yes, I grew up there, and it wasn't. Not really," Isa said quietly, lost in thought.

"But it looks like it was beautiful," Eden pressed.

"Beauty is all about the heart, not the eyes," Isa said, sighing. "It was a cold, lonely place. Now this garage apartment is better. I stayed here after I graduated from college, during the summer I dated Charles. It holds some sweet memories. But the best place of all is right down this driveway to that little house over there."

"My house?" Eden asked.

"Yup, that's where Aunt Ruth lived. Aunt Ruth never married, but boy, did she know how to live! Every time I'd go over she'd have some fun project we'd do together. Not big things. Sometimes it was baking bread or canning berries or putting up some new wacky wallpaper she had found at the five and dime."

"I think most of those wallpapers are still there." Eden remembered the faded yellow paper in the kitchen covered with large bright orange and hot pink daisies of various sizes.

"One summer we even painted the house, and she let me choose the color. She never repainted it. I've called it the blueberry house ever since." Isa looked off in the distance like she was trying to capture those long forgotten years.

"The blueberry house—I like it." Eden paused. "But when we do repaint it, will that be all right with you?"

Isa perked up and leaned forward. "Of course, and you paint it any color you like. A home should be a living, breathing thing. It gets messy; it gets cleaned. It's one color one day and a different the next. The greatest gift you can give that place is to wake it up and throw your arms around it. When you do decide to paint, give me a holler. I'd love to help."

"Well, we'll see." Eden knew they couldn't afford to paint it soon, and here even Isa was expecting it of her. "I've got to go." She stood to leave.

"I understand, you have little ones calling for you, but I need to tell you—how can I say it?" Isa grabbed her white linen skirt and yanked on it. "This is my blank canvas outfit. I was looking for my next inspiration—for some great truth—and here you show up. Thank you for coming. I think I have a lot to learn from you."

As Eden looked toward her house, the peeling blue paint didn't look quite as bad. It seemed like the sagging porch and curling shingles had transformed into something once loved and perhaps a little hopeful. Now it was *Blueberry House.*

16

A Mountain of Dirty Laundry

The steam from the warm cup of coffee wafted up to greet Lisa as she tried to focus on the fourth new case file she had been handed that morning. The sleep deprivation was getting to her, and she had been up all night worrying again. Every mistake haunted her. She'd only been on the job two months, and this had been the fifth one.

It was after eight last Friday evening when the call had come in. The abuse hotline had a unique ring. During the day no one really noticed as calls came in constantly from annoyed neighbors, exes trying to use kids as pawns in custody battles, and overly cautious professionals, but in the evening, things changed.

With each call, the room hushed. Two out of three required immediate attention. She listened as the experienced caseworker took the information, and her stomach had wrenched in knots. She recognized the address. It was a case she had closed a few weeks ago. The child had been sleeping on a recliner, but the two younger siblings toddling around the room seemed to be happy, and the small apartment was impressively tidy.

The references she had talked to said they hadn't heard or seen anything unusual. As trained, her job in the evaluation branch of Family Services only included assessing whether a potential threat could be verified. At that point the file would be escalated to the child protection branch, where more extensive testing would be done to determine whether the case would be handed over to Family Support Services or Temporary Foster Care.

This morning she heard that an ambulance had been dispatched. The boyfriend had come home drunk, and now the oldest child was in critical condition. Lisa couldn't stop thinking about the poor sleeping child she had seen. They said bruises were found all over his body. Why hadn't she insisted they wake him up? Then she might have been able to tell whether something was really wrong.

Her mind honed in on another little boy she had recently investigated. The picture of his little body curled up on the couch while his mother juggled a fussy infant came forcefully to her mind. At the time the house seemed in good order, and she had thought the mother to be a little high-strung, but basically normal. Yet that was what she had thought before, and now that little kid was in ICU. They were saying he might not survive.

Lisa dropped the file she was looking through on her desk and opened her lower drawer, rifling through the twenty open cases she was in the process of investigating. She found the folder, laid the pages open on her desk, and scanned them for any hints between the lines in the police report—something beyond the obvious. The officers mentioned that they had received three complaints of the child running away. In the margin was a simple question, "Why does he run?" Perhaps the officer had sensed something.

She grabbed the Styrofoam cup and headed for the door, determined to keep her eyes open.

•　•　•　•　•

Cath stood at the door and gasped. It was difficult to imagine that two days ago the room had been sparkling. Every article of folded laundry had been put away. Even the socks were matched, and in a sudden moment of victory, she had disposed of the matchless handful that had been bouncing around like wild bachelors for months. But the weekend had a way of spinning things out of control, and she pushed up her sleeves, ready to dive in.

The mountain of towels and sheets from the maze in the backyard added to the massive heap she had accumulated from the bathrooms and hampers throughout the house. It was as though the pile had been rising slowly all weekend like warm bread dough, ready to fill the entire room and ooze down the hall if she didn't pound it down immediately. Even the trash can in the corner was overflowing beyond capacity.

As she stepped through the threshold, the phone rang, and Cath had to admit she was grateful for the reprieve. She ran down the hall. "Hello?"

"Hi, it's Eden." She hesitated. "How's Sandra?"

"Physically or emotionally?" Cath laughed to herself. "I suppose the answer is the same. She's a teenager."

"Oh, then she's all right?"

"Yes." Cath's voice lifted, curious why she was asking. "What can I do for you, Eden?"

"I hate to call, but I've got a favor to ask you."

"Really? I can't believe my ears."

"Why?" Eden swallowed.

"Because you're actually asking me for something. This is a first." Cath laughed.

"Well, I didn't know who else to call. My mother's helped out with watching the kids before, but with two. . ." She paused. "The truth is, she could barely handle me."

"So, you want me to watch the children? How wonderful!"

"Just Hayden. I've got a doctor's appointment this morning that I totally forgot about, and I don't dare miss it."

"Double wonderful! I could really use the help today. How is he at doing laundry?"

"Are you serious?" Eden asked.

"Yup, and be grateful you don't know how serious I am." Cath covered her forehead as she thought of the disaster upstairs. "What time can you bring him over?"

"In fifteen minutes? Sorry, I told you I forgot," she said softly.

"Triple wonderful! The hardest part of being home after your children are in school is that it's the same amount of work—laundry, meal planning, and housecleaning—without the company. I'm thrilled he'll be here—the sooner the better."

Cath put down the receiver and skipped down the hall. She would get the first load in before Hayden got there, and then they could make sock puppets. She hurried over to the trash can and yanked out the pile of unmatched socks she had discarded the Wednesday before.

• • • • •

Marlene's doorbell rang. She peeked through the little window to the side of the door to see a floppy gardening hat.

"Helen." She opened the door. "What can I do for you?"

"I'm here to gather extra collections for a special neighborhood beautification project."

"I don't remember discussing anything like that at the last home-owners' meeting."

"Oh, I was only recently informed of it myself," Helen said meekly. "I hate to get people's hopes up because if we can't raise an extra three thousand dollars, it won't even be a possibility. But I can tell you this, it's a construction project that will transform the face of the entire street."

Marlene clapped her hands together. "Did the bid come in on the curbs and sidewalks?"

"I can't say, but I know you'll be pleased. Now you can pay with cash, check, or I just happen to have credit card slips in my purse."

Marlene reached in her pocket for her credit card, thinking she could offer a few hundred dollars, as an unfamiliar car pulled into her driveway. A young woman walked up to them with a clipboard.

"We don't want any." Marlene dismissed the girl before returning to her conversation.

"Excuse me," the young woman said, undeterred. "I'm Lisa Walker, a social worker from the state. Are you Marlene Thomas?"

"Oh, I totally forgot. Eden told me you'd be coming."

"I am currently investigating allegations against your neighbor and was wondering if you could answer a few questions."

Helen lifted herself to her full five-foot-ten height. "I live right across the street from her. Could I be of service?"

"Yes, I could use your input as well." Lisa smiled and turned to Marlene. "To start off, can you tell me your general feelings about what's going on over there?"

Marlene thought about Eden and began to feel a little sorry for her. She had judged her too harshly, but Hayden's escaping was a huge problem. The caseworker tapped on her clipboard impatiently, but

Marlene wasn't sure what to say and for once stayed quiet.

Helen cleared her throat. "Perhaps I can shed some light on the situation. Exactly seven months ago that family moved in across the street. When they first arrived, everything was acceptable, but then she had her baby. At that point all hell broke loose. Their little boy started to run away, and the mother didn't even notice. I found him wandering around all the time. He could have been out for hours, and when I brought him back, she didn't even seem to care. I think she had been asleep."

A woman who runs down the street after a toddler in only a towel definitely cares about him being out, Marlene thought and opened her mouth to interject as another car pulled in front, and Hillary jumped out.

"Oh, I'm sorry," Hillary said stopping midway down the walk. "I didn't realize you have company. Marlene, can you call me? It's really important."

If it was anything else, Marlene would have dropped everything to find out what was going on because the expression on Hillary's face was frantic, but this problem with Eden was important. She waved a bangled arm. "I promise I'll call you as soon as I can, Hillary."

Lisa's head popped up. "Hillary? Hillary Jacobs?"

"Yes?" Hillary answered.

"I'm from Family Protective Services." A smile lit up the young woman's face. "It seems more than coincidence that three references would be here at the same time," she said, shaking her head.

"No, I've got to—" Hillary backed away.

"It will only take a minute. It says here that you watch Hayden Duncan on Sundays?"

"Hayden? You're asking about Hayden?" She gave a nervous laugh. "Well, all right. Yes, I remember Eden mentioning it. Yes, she told me what to tell you." Hillary closed her eyes and bit her lip before beginning. "Hayden is fine. When he is in my care, I have never seen a single problem."

The words came out wooden and sounded so insincere it made Marlene blink. What was Hillary doing?

Lisa turned to her suspiciously. "How long have you known the mother?"

"Years—at least three or four," Hillary answered quickly.

"Do you consider her a friend?" Lisa asked, her head tilted to one side.

"Of course, we're very close." Hillary plastered a too big smile across her face and spoke through it. "Do you need anything else? I've got to go."

The caseworker wrote some notes on her clipboard and stared at Hillary, making her physically squirm. Lisa shook her head and stuck her hand in one of her jacket pockets to retrieve a business card. "If you think of anything else that might help this investigation, would you please call me? Our concern is for the child. Do you understand?"

"Yes, ma'am." Hillary grabbed the card and rushed back to her car as though she was being chased.

·　·　·　·　·

Her fingers shook as she tried to fit the key into the ignition. Finally, it went in, and she turned on the car and floored the gas, screeching away into the street.

Hillary turned the corner, scanning the distance for any sign of him. She had hoped that Marlene would help look too, but now she was on her own. She couldn't lose him. Just last year her older son, Zeniff, had done the same thing, and she'd never seen him again. It would kill her to lose Cory. As she passed the gas station, she began to sob with relief.

He sat on the edge of the curb by the pay phone. She pulled up, and without lifting his head, he opened the door and got in. She looked at his face. There was a wide red mark at the top of his cheek that looked like it might bruise.

"Cory, you have to be more careful. When you get him upset . . ."

"Don't, Mom." He hit the dashboard with his fist. "Don't make excuses for him."

There was nothing left to say. Mother and son drove home in empty silence.

17

More than You'll Ever Know

Lisa left Marlene's house more confused than ever. It was clear Helen was not enamored with her neighbor, and Marlene admitted Eden was struggling but thought the situation was improving. It was Hillary's strange reaction that had her stumped. She was obviously covering something up. Perhaps the situation would become clearer with the last reference—Kimberly Parker.

She rang the doorbell and knocked twice, but no one was home. Marching back to the car, Lisa made a decision. She would pass this case on for further testing. She had three references and a home visit and couldn't with a clear conscience let it go. No, it warranted further investigation, and with the workload piling up on her desk, her best option was to let Child Protection take over.

• • • • •

As Eden drove out to the highway toward her doctor's appointment, she couldn't get over the fact that Hayden seemed as happy as Cath to be left at her house to play. It should have been a relief, but guilt for lying to Cath left her uncomfortable. She hadn't forgotten about the appointment at all, but she couldn't call her mother.

After their last conversation, she wasn't sure she ever wanted to speak to her again. *Mom will never understand my life. Maybe it's better if we each go our separate ways.* Eden sighed. She pulled into the parking lot and grabbed Miley's car seat. As she stepped into the full waiting room, she realized that it had taken much less time than expected, and she was twenty minutes early.

Eden found a quiet corner behind a large plant, grabbed some fun gossip magazines, and began reading. She was thoroughly engrossed in who had been caught wearing the same dress at the last academy awards when she looked up to see Kimberly marching out of the office.

She jumped up and stood right in front of her. "Kimberly, I didn't know you come here too."

"This is my first, and probably my *last*, visit to this establishment." Kimberly clutched her sleek leather purse with such force that the firm sides were collapsing in. "Excuse me, I've got to go."

Eden wasn't sure if Kimberly's anger was directed at the doctor or her, but it didn't matter. She had to talk to her, and this could be her last opportunity. "There is something very important I need to discuss with you."

"I'm sorry but—"

Thwack! The door beside the window where the receptionist was sitting was thrown open with such force it hit the wall. A short nurse with a round shining face gushed forward. "Mrs. Parker, you forgot your new baby kit! Congratulations, again."

She tried to hand the designer diaper bag filled with coupons and samples to Kimberly, who stood unmoving, clearly disgusted at the thought.

"How dare you?" Kimberly glared at Eden like it was all her fault and then back at the nurse before she rushed from the room.

The nurse's face fell, but she recovered quickly enough, turning with a huff and muttering to the full waiting room, "It's the hormones." A few people broke into laughter as the nurse toddled away and shut the door behind her.

Eden stood alone in the crowded waiting room with most of the women staring in her direction. Her face reddened as she tried to figure out what had happened.

18
Trying to Understand

By the time Eden drove up to Cath's house, she was more confused than ever. She had played through what happened in the doctor's office so many different ways that it had left her exhausted. Was Kimberly upset with the doctor? Was she mad she was even having a baby, or was she furious at her and wanted to get away? Her stomach ached. She knew that any day now the caseworker would be approaching her. Kimberly had to be told, but Eden didn't want to risk making her even angrier.

As soon as she shut the car door and approached the generous porch, lugging Miley in her carrier, Hayden and Cath appeared at the front door. Hayden had sock puppets on both hands and on each foot One resembled a dog, another a cat, a pig, and a hen—all with googly eyes. He babbled and toddled carefully down the stairs, impeded by his masterpieces. Eden had to smile at the clever way of hobbling her boy who loved to run.

"We had so much fun! Thank you for a great day." Cath chuckled.

"Did you get much laundry done?" Eden asked.

"Not nearly enough, but what else is new? We did make a huge batch of cowboy cookies. Why don't you come in and try some? Hayden broke the eggs all by himself."

"Yes! Yes! Yes!" Hayden grabbed his mother's free hand with his sock-covered ones and tried to drag her toward the door.

"Wow." She smiled at Cath. "He's always saying 'no, no, no' around me. What am I doing wrong?"

"You've got to remember I'm not the mom, just a little window of fun. I had plenty of no's in my day." Cath walked into the kitchen. "As a matter of fact, I still have plenty of no's. You should have been a fly on the wall at breakfast. Sandra was late to seminary again. Why don't you put the car seat on the counter, and we'll sit down, so Hayden can serve us some cookies?"

Eden carefully placed a sleeping Miley, still buckled in her carrier, on the counter. "I don't think you'll ever get those puppets off his hands."

Cath pulled out a paper bag with pictures of each of his puppet friends on the front and a large letter "H" for Hayden. He stuffed the socks in the bag and set it by the door and then, with a little encouragement from Cath, passed out the napkins and cookies. Cath poured the milk, and the three of them sat down to their treat.

"I'm impressed."

"Don't be." Cath bent forward to look past Eden and smile at Hayden. "We practiced about ten times, didn't we?"

Hayden giggled, and Eden couldn't remember seeing him so happy. She knew it should have made her happy too, but instead it seemed like one more illustration of what an awful mother she was. She'd never made crafts with Hayden. She didn't even know he was capable of it, and the only cookie recipe Eden owned was the one on the back of the chocolate chip package.

"You are so lucky. Do you know that?" Cath said, staring at Miley's sleeping face.

"What do you mean?" Eden looked around her at Cath's large, clean home.

"I'd do anything to go back to the time when I had little ones. Every day is an adventure. Every activity is new to them. It's such a fun time."

"Fun?" Eden bit her cookie. "That's not how I'd describe it."

"Oh, I know it's a lot of hard work, but wait until they're teenagers—it gets easier in a way. Seriously, Eden, remember that you're doing the work of eternity. I think of all those little angels in heaven waiting to come to earth to kind, loving families and how many women aren't brave enough to invite them into their homes. You're remarkable."

"No, not me." Eden thought about the caseworker and wished she could tell Cath but didn't dare.

"Just look at that sweet face." Cath's eyes were riveted on the infant as Miley slept. The baby's fair hair glistened in the sunlight. "I know that now it may seem like each day lasts forever, but in a breath they're grown up. My baby is at school all day long now. He'll never be mine the same way again. I so miss having a baby of my own."

"Why don't you have another? You aren't that old." Eden couldn't help but ask.

Cath paused and then stood and threw away her napkin. Hayden was getting wiggly, and Eden wondered if it was time to go.

"He can go play in the other room. Hayden knows where the toy basket is," Cath suggested.

Eden let him down, and he bustled into the back room.

Cath came and sat next to her again. "Do you really want to know the answer to that question?"

Eden fiddled with her napkin. "I suppose it's your own business, and I shouldn't have asked. I mean, like, I saw Kimberly at the doctor's office. You'd think she'd be thrilled about expecting her first baby, but she acted really upset. I guess people have their reasons, and I should just stay out of it."

Cath touched her arm. "I don't think so. The way we become sisters is by sharing each other's lives, not by pushing each other away." She leaned back in her chair. "When I had Mike, I had some serious complications and became very anemic. The doctor thought it best if I waited a few years before having any more. Now I'm well over thirty. I'm almost too old."

"That's funny." Eden closed her eyes. "My mom wanted me to wait until at least thirty to have children at all, so I could have a life first. She flipped out when I had Hayden and hasn't come over to see Miley at all, even though she lives right in town."

"That's got to be hard. I know a lot of people thought I was crazy for having four right off the bat, but I wouldn't change it for anything in the world."

A crash from the other room sent both women hurrying into the back where Hayden stood with the upturned basket over his head. "No, Hayden," Eden corrected her son.

Cath shrugged and sat beside him on the floor. "Hey, can you do this?" She threw a toy in the basket. He did too. Cath grabbed another and chucked it in. So did Hayden. Soon the basket was full, and the sounds of the baby beginning to rouse made Eden anxious to get home.

"Thanks so much. You really helped me out in a bind," Eden said later as she buckled Hayden in his car seat with his "H" bag of puppets clasped tightly to his chest.

* * * * *

Cath waved as the car pulled away and shut the front door behind her. "The truth is, you helped me more than you'll ever know."

19

True Motivations

Two days later she had done it. Everything was clean. Cath juggled the large bundle of folded shirts and jeans in her arms. She jogged down the hall, turned on point, and rushed to her closet. Placing the clothes on the shelf, she bolted out the door to get the next pile when something pulled her back. Out of the corner of her eye, she caught a glimpse of the sleeve of a plaid polyester suit wedged in the back of the closet. Remembering the Nerd Party coming up that evening, she took it with her to the laundry room.

The things this suit has seen. She shook her head and laughed to herself. Holding the bright orange and tan plaid suit with decorative stitching in front of her brought an entire era to her mind. Large hoop earrings, white lipstick, teased hair, disco music, miniskirts made semi-modest with heavy tights. She remembered her older sisters being in the thick of it, though things had calmed down a little by the time she was a teenager.

Cath turned the washing machine knob to delicate, gently laid the suit around the agitator of her Maytag, and closed the lid. As she did, a song came to mind. She hadn't heard it since she was a freshman in high school. Her first year in seminary was on the Book of Mormon, and their teacher played this tape over and over. The chorus came back to her immediately.

Heed Moroni's promise.
Pray and search it through,
And the Spirit will bear witness
That the Book of Mormon's true.

She tried to recall the other words, but her mind drew a blank. Cath grabbed Carson's pile of clothes and attempted to focus on the things she needed to accomplish that afternoon, but the forgotten words kept annoying her. *What are they? If I could only remember the first line, the others would come to me.*

With the laundry done, Cath ran downstairs to the basement. A few random thoughts that started with the ugly suit had morphed into an entire event with the family, that is, if she could find the right box. *I wonder if the kids will mind having an emergency Saturday morning FHE.*

• • • • •

Hayden sat in the corner playing happily with his hand puppets. The dog was missing his eyes, but the others were holding up quite nicely. Isa had been impressed with his treasures and had found a large cardboard box that she painted like a theatre. She set it in the corner of her studio where Hayden was playing now.

Miley lay asleep in her stroller, and Eden sat awkwardly on the stool, feeling terribly uncomfortable.

"Are you sure this is all right? Or should I sit like this?" She twisted her legs to the other side of the chair and held her head at an angle.

Isa sighed. "It really doesn't matter as long as you relax and act natural. I'm not going to bite." She stood before a large easel with paintbrush and pallet in hand, quickly dabbing and swirling the paint on the canvas.

"Hello! Anybody home?" Kimberly stuck her head through the door. "Sorry for the intrusion."

Isa looked delighted and put down her work. "Two visitors in one day. What a treat!"

"I was looking for Eden." She glanced around the room and then saw her in the chair. "There you are. Do you know you left your front door open?"

"What is anyone going to steal?" Eden stood and hurried to stop Hayden from retrieving Isa's pallet and continuing her painting for her.

"I don't know. You've got to keep an eye out for that neighbor of yours. I think she's beginning to lose it, if you know what I mean." Kimberly pointed to her head and rolled her eyes.

Isa laughed with glee. "That Helen is too ornery to lose anything. She'll be sharp as a tack until she's one hundred, I bet."

"I don't know. She said something about Eden redoing her whole house by next week. I thought you said it would be a while."

"Something like that." Eden hefted Hayden on her hip. She gripped the stroller and turned it toward the door. "I've got to go, Isa, before Miley wakes up. Thanks for the fun morning."

"Are you sure?" Isa pouted.

"We'll talk tomorrow," Eden assured her and made a beeline for the door. Both of the other women followed.

"I'll go with you," Kimberly volunteered.

Eden paused, looked at her, and took a deep breath. She'd been trying to avoid it, but she really needed to talk to Kimberly, and now was as good a time as any. "All right. Thank you, Isa." She waved to Isa as they walked out the door.

Hayden rushed on ahead as Kimberly and Eden walked side by side. "Hey, it feels like old times, doesn't it?" Kimberly gave a wan smile.

"Huh?" Eden looked at her companion, confused.

"You know, walking group?" Kimberly clarified.

"Oh, yeah, walking group." She paused and then decided she didn't really care anymore. "You know, Marlene told me I killed it."

Kimberly burst out laughing. "Marlene *would* say something like that—so dramatic. No, I think walking group had a major fatal flaw, and by the time you joined, it was sort of on its last legs anyway."

"What flaw are you talking about?" Eden asked.

"Me."

Eden paused. "Really?"

Kimberly kept on walking. "I had a hard time appreciating it. I need to apologize to you. I'm so sorry—"

"Wait, why are you apologizing?" Eden covered her mouth. "You didn't do what I think you did. What did you say to her?"

"To whom?"

"The caseworker. Oh, Kimberly, what have you done?"

Kimberly shook her head at her friend's distress. "I haven't talked to anyone."

Eden tried to calm herself. "You see, we're being investigated by the state because of Hayden running away, and I put you down as a reference. I thought you had—"

"Helen." Kimberly scowled. "Why that old battle ax, I can't believe she'd stoop that low."

"Believe it." Eden pushed the stroller faster and began to hurry since Hayden had passed her house and was continuing up the street.

Kimberly jogged ahead, and as she approached Hayden, he hurried back to his mom and hugged her leg. Kimberly walked back too. "I wanted to apologize about what happened in the doctor's office," Kimberly said. "I wanted to explain."

"Why don't you come on in?"

• • • • •

Cath stuffed another cowboy cookie in her mouth without thinking and scribbled down the words of the song playing on the old Fisher Price tape recorder. In the age of CDs and iPods, it had taken more time to find something to play it on than to find the tape itself.

> *Their eyes are not yet opened for they cannot see the truth.*
> *The book for them was written as a guide for wandering youth,*
> *So help us read that we may see the answer to our prayers,*
> *That we may know within our hearts the truth of all that's there.*

Finished, she set down the pencil and looked at the clock again, surprised the children weren't home yet. Then she remembered she'd forgotten to set the clock back two weeks earlier for daylight saving time. With another hour to go, she looked at the cookie in her hand. *I'm already squeezing into my fat jeans and refuse to grow another size.* She peeked in the teddy bear jar and scowled—there were still over a dozen left.

Well, maybe there's someone who needs those cookies right now. I can do an act of service and withstand temptation at the same time. She put down the half-eaten cookie, ran to the little cupboard beside the dining room, and got out a Tupperware container filled with ribbons. In a few minutes she had a cute little package ready to deliver. Wracking her brain, she suddenly remembered that Eden had said something about Kimberly expecting a baby.

Kimberly would be one of those mothers who raised Olympic athletes and Nobel Prize winners. Cath was sure of it. She wrote a short note saying as much, tucked it under the ribbon, and jumped in the car to run it over to her. The third time she knocked, Cath had to admit Kimberly wasn't home. She was surprised because Kimberly's car was there, but she could have gone somewhere with her husband. Deciding it was meant to be, Cath got back in the car to eat the cookies after all. She took the note off the package, laid it beside her on the passenger seat, and began untying the ribbon when she heard someone calling her name.

"Cath, Cath." Marlene ran over to the car while Cath rolled down her window. "We finished the decorations for the party tonight, and I think you're going to *love it*." She almost sang her last two words.

Cath straightened the bow and held out the package, feeling caught in the act. "Marlene, you're timing is perfect. I came to deliver this to Kimberly. She's expecting a baby, and so I thought chocolate was probably an appropriate gift."

"Finally! I wondered if they were ever going to start a family. How did you find out?"

"Eden ran into her at the doctor's office. I think we're some of the first to know."

Marlene hugged the package and smiled. "That's what visiting teachers are for."

20

Spoiled Secrets

Kimberly stepped through the door and fiddled with her hands. She fidgeted as she waited for Eden to unbuckle the baby from the stroller and open a bin of action figures for Hayden to play with. Finally, Eden settled in the rocking chair and invited Kimberly to sit as well.

Watching her hold the sweet infant, Kimberly put a protective hand over her abdomen and dreamt that soon it could be her. "Tell me something. The first time you met me, what did you think?"

"I thought you were amazing," Eden said.

"No, you didn't. Be honest. What did you think when you found out I didn't have kids yet?"

"I don't know." Eden smoothed her hand across Miley's soft sleeper.

"Oh, come off it." Kimberly couldn't sit anymore and began pacing around. "You wondered if I had put off having kids for a career or if I even liked kids at all. Everybody does. It drives me crazy."

Eden lowered her eyes, feeling guilty for entertaining such thoughts herself. "I understand."

"No, I don't think you do. Brent and I have been married for eight years. The first five years we simply never got pregnant. I was working for a brokerage company and doing quite well, so I didn't worry about it for a while. Then three years ago, we found out we were expecting."

"Really?" Eden listened intently.

"The same week I found out, I lost him. My doctor told me it was

96

nothing out of the ordinary. He said to keep going—business as usual. Last year I got pregnant again and lost that one too." She paused.

"How awful." Eden shook her head slightly.

"Yeah, it was. That time the doc suggested it was the stress of my job. So, when Brent was transferred, I quit, and we moved here."

"At least that's good, and now you're expecting, like you wanted," Eden offered.

"The only problem is that this time I've got my eyes open. My last doctor didn't do any tests to find out what the root cause of the miscarriages was. When I found out that I was expecting for sure, I realized what a fool I'd been. I thought there was no way this baby would make it to term."

"I'm so sorry." Eden stopped rocking and searched Kimberly's eyes with concern.

"Don't be." Kimberly sat on the edge of the couch. "The bishop got back in town last week and came by last night to give me a blessing. As he lifted his hands off my head, I was filled with peace. It's going to be okay." Her shoulders relaxed.

"What a relief." Eden leaned back and began rocking the baby again.

"Yeah, it was remarkable. He said I would find motherhood to be the most rewarding career of my life. That's a pretty tall order, considering how great my last job was." She closed her eyes and seemed to drift away.

"Interesting—to find motherhood your most rewarding career. What a unique way to put it." Eden wondered if she found motherhood to be rewarding. *It's certainly overwhelming and exhausting, but rewarding?*

Kimberly stood, walked forward, and then knelt before Miley and took her little hand in her own. "It was a great blessing, but the other thing I felt as soon as the bishop left was that I needed to talk to you. I'm sorry I was so rude at the doctor's office. I had a lot on my mind."

"I totally understand."

"Can I ask you one more thing?" Kimberly lowered her gaze. "Please don't tell anybody about this in case this one doesn't make it. I don't want the whole ward feeling sorry for me, you know?"

"I do." Eden imagined an aversion to pity must be something they had in common. "I totally understand. I haven't told anybody about my issues with the state except the people I asked to be references. I don't even think the bishop knows."

"So we're okay?" Kimberly headed for the door.

"Yeah." Eden laid her hand on her chest. "I'm so relieved. I thought you were really mad at me."

"Why would I be mad at you?"

"For killing the walking group, for having you search for Hayden that one time—you looked really upset that morning."

"Not upset—jealous. You've got everything I want. It's hard for me not to turn green every once in a while. Sorry."

"Are you kidding? Look around. We've got nothing. If one more person asks me when we're going to fix up our house, I'm going to scream." Eden couldn't believe the words had escaped her mouth, but it felt good to let them go.

"About that . . ." Kimberly swallowed. "You know, since I've moved here, I've been incredibly underwhelmed. I was looking at your house and would love to start listing what needs improvement. The structure is surprisingly sound. The foundation looks impeccable, and there doesn't seem to be any water issues at all. Would you mind if I inspected it more closely and developed a plan to fix it up?"

"Why?" Eden eyed her suspiciously.

"Because it needs to be done." Kimberly shrugged. "I bet you could get the labor really cheap with the economic slump, and the supplies might not be nearly as much as you think. Maybe I simply want to do something for you, and I don't bake." She held her lips straight across in an expectant smile.

The Relief Society president's words rang through Eden's mind, and she wondered if sometimes service consisted of allowing someone else to help you. She nodded. "It actually might be fun to plan, even if it is years before I can do anything. It's a deal."

Two hours later Kimberly strolled down the road and noticed the leaves on the large oak at the end of the cul-de-sac beginning to edge with red and gold. As she turned to her right to head home, she couldn't stop herself from humming. The papers in her hands rustled, and she scanned through the complete list of needed repairs for each room. Her eyes raced over the words again, and her mind started categorizing the level of each task. She picked up her pace and found she was dying to get to the phone when a sound made her stop.

"Kimberly, I've got something for you!" Marlene waved a box above her head and hurried to catch up. Kimberly turned and rolled her eyes. She hid the list behind her back, determined to respect Eden's privacy.

"What is it?" She prepared to endure another of Marlene's senseless tirades.

"I've got a present for you." Marlene scrunched up her face unnaturally. "I've heard the news. Congratulations."

"What news?" Kimberly's face was expressionless.

Marlene reached out and touched Kimberly's flat stomach. "You know, the baby? It's so exciting." She jiggled her shoulders back and forth.

Kimberly felt sick. "How did you find out?" Her mind was going a mile a minute. Surely, the bishop would have kept her confidence.

"Oh, I heard that Eden ran into you at the doctor's office. Now, if there is anything I can do . . ."

"You've done quite enough." Kimberly grabbed the box and marched toward home. *Why hadn't Eden told her that she had already spilled her secret? And not just to anyone but to the biggest gossip in the entire ward?* She folded up the papers and shoved them in her pocket.

21

A Change of Plans

The freshly washed plaid leisure suit looked brand new. Cath hung it on a sturdy wooden hanger and was carrying it back to her room when she heard footsteps on the stairs.

"Mom?" Sandra rounded the corner and stopped short. "Gross! You still have that thing?"

"Till the day I die." Cath hung the outfit tenderly on the back of the door, remembering her first dance with Kevin. The suit was so outdated that the handsome engineer repelled most of the girls, leaving an opportunity that she never regretted.

"At least I already know who'll win the nerd contest and the pie in the face." Sandra collapsed on the bed.

"I don't." Cath raised her eyebrows. "I heard from Jerri that the bishop has some pretty scary duds himself."

"What about Brother Beckman? Do you think he'll dress up? I can't imagine him in anything but black pants and a white shirt."

"Well." Cath laughed. "If he doesn't dress up, maybe that makes him the biggest nerd of all."

Sandra popped up to a sitting position and shook her head. "No way, Mom. Brother Beckman won't win."

"Why not?"

"Because no one's brave enough to throw a pie at him." The visual picture made them both giggle.

Cath hurried into the bathroom to start getting ready, and Sandra followed her and sat on the counter. "Mom?"

"Uh-huh," she said while putting freckles on her nose with the eyebrow pencil.

"Do you know if Eden's going to the party?"

Cath tilted her head to think. "I don't remember her mentioning it, and that's Sister Duncan to you."

"Come on, Mom. She's like five years older than me." Sandra dropped a lipstick on the counter and folded her arms. "You really are stuck-up."

"It's not about being stuck-up. It's about respect." Cath looked into her daughter's eyes and scrunched up her nose. "Okay, so it's your choice what you call her. Now why did you want to know about Eden?"

With her mom's complete attention, Sandra sat forward. "Well, I bet she thinks she can't go because of the baby and her little boy. He's really not that bad. I don't blame him for running out of nursery. If Sister Jacobs were my teacher, I'd run out too."

"I think you already do." Her mom gave her a knowing smile as she put on the bright orange lipstick they had argued about the week before.

"Brother Bowen is so boring!" Sandra grabbed the lipstick and began spinning the tube up and down. "Besides, Eden's the only one with a baby in the ward, and she spends a lot of time in the mother's lounge by herself. I think she's lonely."

Looking at her daughter, Cath smiled. She was proud to see her focusing on others and had wondered the same thing. "I think it'd be a great idea to call her and offer to babysit. Why don't you have them come over here? Hayden had a fun time the other day. Your brothers could play with him while you took care of that precious Miley."

"You sure he'd be safe?" Sandra froze, her face filled with doubt. "The boys play rough."

"I'm pretty sure you'll keep them in line." Cath grabbed some ponytail holders and pulled her bangs in a big pigtail on the top of her head, which shot straight up in the air like a fountain.

"Wow, Mom."

"What?"

"You sure are giving Dad a run for his money on this nerd thing." As Sandra hurried out the door, she paused, wondering if she should talk to her mom about the other thing too. Shaking it off, she hurried to the phone.

•   •   •   •   •

Sitting at the spotless glass-topped dinette, Helen watched as the minute hand hit the twelve and then she began dialing. Time was up. She had said two weeks, and if action took three days like it had the last time, then she was within her rights to move forward. "Child Protective Services? I have some information that may be of interest . . ."

22

An Unexpected Detour

When Josh walked in the door, he hardly recognized his wife. She was wearing a floral shirt with plaid capris and hiking boots. She had thickened and united her eyebrows, applied an explosion of blue eye shadow, and smeared hot pink lipstick all over her mouth.

"Whoa! What happened to you?" he recoiled.

"Josh." She pouted. "Didn't you get my message? The nerd party starts in twenty minutes. The Reeds called and offered to watch the children at their house."

"And you're taking them up on it?" he asked surprised.

"Well, Sandra's great with the baby, and they've got three boys to handle Hayden." She turned back into the room and packed up the last of the diaper bag. "With four babysitters, I think they'll be okay."

"What alien came and took over my wife?" Josh poked her with his index finger. "You look—dare I say it—happy."

"Well, I had a great day. Isa's painting my picture, and Kimberly came over. We had a nice talk. She wants to do a profile on the house and estimate repairs. The list isn't nearly as long as I thought."

"Wait a minute. I knew that smile was going to cost me."

"I know we won't be able to do anything for a while, but it will give us a ballpark idea of what we need to save for. Besides, you're up for your review next month, and with all the hours you're putting in, Cal has to give you a raise."

Josh moaned. "Cal doesn't have to do anything. You know what he told us today? He sold those extra components to another distributor.

They're no good without the transistors, so now we have that order and all our back orders that are already late. He's burning everyone out. Three more people quit today."

"I'm so sorry. Do you think your job is in danger?"

"Cal needs me. I'm the only engineer in the world that would put up with his junk. The question is how long I'm willing to do it. He's running this company to the ground. What good are short-term sales when you don't meet your obligations to your bread-and-butter customers? These specials can't be making more than the cost of training new line workers. He's such a . . . nerd! Hey, maybe we should invite him to the party!"

"I've been thinking the same thing all day but about Isa."

"That's not very nice. I thought you were friends." Josh looked confused.

"Not that she's a nerd, but that I should invite her." She rushed to the bathroom, put away her makeup bag, and straightened up the counter. "I've barely gotten to know her and don't want to seem like a religious fanatic, ya know?" She looked up at Josh, who was eyeing the bed. "Don't you dare lie down. You get dressed while I pack up the car. We'll leave in ten minutes."

Eden went to check on the children one more time. Both were still napping, so she headed out the front door with the neatly packed diaper bag. On the way back to the house, she spied the mailbox and decided to grab the mail. The sky was growing dim. She leafed through the three-inch pile of junk mail, as she walked in the door, almost passing the letter from State Family Services. Once she realized what it was, she dropped the rest of the pile on the kitchen table and ripped open the envelope. As she read the words, she gripped the chair beside her for balance.

"I can't believe it. How dare she?"

Josh shot out of the room with his polka dotted shirt half buttoned. "What is it?"

"They've escalated our case. This is awful." Her mouth hung open, and she threw the letter at him.

He read it quickly. "It only says they're investigating and haven't decided anything yet."

"Did you look in the corner?" She jabbed the paper so hard he almost dropped it. "Three unsatisfactory reports. Do you know what that means?" Eden face grew red. "It means she lied."

"Who?" Josh was confused.

"Kimberly." Eden shook her head. "I'd expect it from Marlene, and Hillary has nothing nice to say about anyone, but Kimberly? She told me she didn't—" Her mind began to race as she replayed the afternoon's events.

"What?" Josh was clueless as to what she was thinking.

"She never did deny it. I asked her about what she said to the caseworker, and she said she didn't know anything about it and changed the subject." She looked around the room. "That crock about not having enough to do and needing a project was probably just a way to get more dirt on us to throw at the state." She sunk down on the sofa in shock.

"Sweetie, you're overreacting. There's no point in worrying about this until we have more information. In the morning we'll call and find out the details."

"It's the weekend."

"Monday morning then. It'll be fine; you'll see." He rushed into the bathroom and soon hopped back into the hall, sporting a freshly gelled alfalfa sprout at the back of his head. "What do you think?"

"You don't want to know." Eden got up with her expression cold as stone and marched to the children's rooms to wake them up so they could leave. She could pretend for two hours that everything was all right, but deep inside there were issues that could no longer be ignored.

· · · · ·

Flora Rodriguez had planned on leaving the office early. It was now after six. She had been out all morning with an emergency intervention and had spent the afternoon double-checking past references and reviewing and highlighting older reports so the case would be airtight. She hoped the judge would finally terminate parental rights this time. The sight of that poor beaten child still made her stomach wretch.

As the last page was sucked through the fax machine, she jammed her copies in the folder and hurried back to her desk to drop them off before heading home. When the phone rang, she kicked herself for answering it. "Flora Rodriguez—Child Protection Branch."

"Oh, I was looking for Lisa. I'm calling about the Duncan situation. I'm from the homeowners' association." The voice on the line was faint, and Flora guessed that the woman was trying to slightly disguise her identity.

"The case has been reassigned to me. May I help you?" Flora had browsed through the file that morning and frankly wondered why it hadn't been dismissed.

"It has come to our attention that the house that family is living in was condemned almost a year ago. I felt it my duty to inform you."

"Hmm." Flora grabbed a pen and wrote a quick note, cradling the phone between her shoulder and her chin. "Are you certain?"

"The documentation is in their file at city hall. I've seen it with my own eyes."

"I'll have to verify it, but if what you say is true, that takes care of that." She yanked the file and put it in her outbox.

"Excuse me?" the caller asked.

"Kids can't live in a condemned house. I'll send a citation as soon as we have the paperwork. They'll have seventy-two hours to evacuate. Case closed."

Hanging up the phone, Flora smiled. On Monday morning she'd make a few calls, and it would be a problem for Family Support to deal with.

23

Who's the Biggest Nerd?

As the car sped down the road, Eden was getting more irritated. Finally, she couldn't take it anymore. "Stop the car. We've got to go back."

Josh applied the brakes and pulled over in the dark. "What is it? Did you leave the baby's bottle? The diaper bag's right there." He did a U-turn and headed toward home.

"No, it's not that."

"You're not going to bug out, are you?" he asked getting ready to pull into their driveway. "There's no point in worrying about something until you can do something about it."

His words stung, but there was something pressing on her even more intensely. She knew she had to do this—whether she wanted to or not. "No, keep going. I've got to invite Isa to the party."

Josh looked at her out of the corner of his eye. "Isn't this a little last minute? Like, aren't we already late?"

"I know. Up there." She pointed for him to pull in behind the little garage. "I'll just be a minute."

Eden hopped out of the car, rapped at the freshly painted fuchsia door, and folded her arms, hoping no one would answer. The entire ride she'd been trying to worry about the state investigation, trying to blame people for saying horrible things about her, and all she could think about was Isa. It shocked her that the Spirit could almost scream at you when it wanted to. Wasn't it supposed to be the still, small voice?

The promptings of the Spirit had done something else too. For the first time, she knew that somehow if she would follow them, she'd be all right. Since right now the Spirit was prompting her to invite her neighbor to this silly nerd party, she reached out and knocked on the door again. She was ready to leave when the door opened.

"Hi, what a nice surprise! Your picture is turning out incredibly well." Isa stood there with a rainbow bandana on her head smudged with paint. Her shirt was an explosion of ruffles in every color, and her pants looked like old-fashioned bloomers in electric blue. On her feet were flip flops that sported huge silk sunflowers that hid most of her toes.

"I know this may seem odd, but we're having a party at our church called a nerd party. It's sort of like a costume party where you dress up like a nerd. Do you want to come?" She twirled her poky pigtail and smiled.

Isa's eyes sparkled. "I'd love to. I can't remember the last time I went to a party. Let me close up my studio, and I'll be right there." She ran away and then turned back, grinning broadly. "At least I won't have to change."

The surprise on Josh's face was evident as the two women made their way to the car. Isa gingerly hopped between the car seats in the back, and they were off.

"So you're the artist I keep hearing about." Josh smiled through the rearview mirror and tried to make small talk. "We have another artist who should be there tonight. She's the one that's hardly ever in town. You know, Eden, she designs children's wards in hospitals."

"Oh yeah, Pattie Beckman. Do you know her?" Eden turned around in her seat.

"Could that be Pattie Wilson? Did she run the daycare?" Isa cocked her head. "Did she get married?"

"Yes, last year she married and joined the Church the same day. Her husband used to be a policeman."

"I can't believe it." Isa beamed. "I helped her flesh out her design on the care center and later painted her house. We even took some art classes together at the university. I love Pattie."

"Well, you'll see her tonight." Josh slapped the steering wheel, smiling.

Miley grabbed Isa's finger and was trying to suck on it, which made Isa's face wrinkle up in glee. "This night will be filled with happy surprises," Isa whispered to the baby.

. . . . .

They arrived at the Reeds as Cath and Kevin were getting in the car. Josh grabbed the baby's car seat and went inside while Eden introduced Isa, who agreed to ride over to the church with the Reeds, since settling the children would take a few minutes. Eden was relieved that poor Isa wouldn't have to sit in the back seat among crushed Cheerios all the way to church and waved good-bye to the carload as she escorted Hayden up the front steps.

She wasn't ten feet from the door when the three boys descended on them. "Hey, Hayden, do you remember me?" Jordan asked, waving.

Mike hurried to Hayden's side and grabbed his hand. "No, Hayden's *my* friend. Want to see my Power Ranger collection?" They bounded up the stairs in a huddle. As an afterthought, Carson went up to Josh and said, "You can come too."

Josh shrugged. "Well, just for a minute." The two ran upstairs to join the festivities.

Sandra was in the kitchen holding the baby, and Eden wandered in toward her. "Are you going to be all right?"

"We'll be fine." She cradled Miley in her arms with practiced ease.

"I think you'll find everything you need in the diaper bag. Any questions?" Eden smiled.

"Just one." She bit her lip. "I've been thinking a lot about what you said."

"About that." Eden moved a step away and put a hand on the counter to steady herself. "I worry I didn't say the right things."

"Maybe not." Sandra's expression was hard. "But it made me think about how much of my life is based on assumptions. I don't really know much of anything. Maybe part of growing up is only acting on things we're sure about."

"Maybe." Eden wasn't certain what she meant but noticed how sad Sandra had become. "You okay?"

"Yeah." Miley began to fuss, and Sandra stuck out her tongue and made a funny noise. The baby laughed, breaking the mood.

Josh appeared at the door. "All ready?"

"I guess." Eden walked around the island and took one look back. "You sure you're all right?"

"Yeah," Sandra said softly and hugged the baby. "But my parents won't be."

24

Foot Twins

As Cath walked into the cultural hall, she had to laugh. Marlene had been in charge of decorations and used the centerpieces that were leftover from a friend's wedding. The light blue fake flowers in amber glass pots, covered with spray glue and glitter, looked like a flower arrangement from *Little Shop of Horrors*. Cath was sure she had seen each of the items at the dollar store. If nerdy was what they were going for, Marlene had certainly succeeded.

Isa seemed to be having a great time welcoming everyone in the room. She chatted in the corner with a portion of the activities committee, and the three elderly ladies were delighted by Isa's attention.

Cath moved over to them and caught Isa's arm. "I hope you don't mind if I steal her back. It looks like we're starting." Cath guided her guest to the center table where Kevin was already sitting. Suddenly Isa let out a shriek, followed by an equivalent yelp across the room.

Pattie ran forward and hugged her friend. "Isa? What are you doing here?"

"Pattie, you're more beautiful than ever. I can't believe it's been so long." Isa kissed her cheek. "And this must be your husband."

Ralph stepped forward and bowed slightly.

"I love you already." Isa hugged him, linked an arm with each of them, and headed toward Cath. "Now, tell me everything. How is Gwen? Is she still at that home?"

Pattie looked down. "She died last year, but the funeral was beautiful, and we had some wonderful conversations there at the end."

"I'm so sorry." Isa paused. "She was a great lady. But what is this I hear about you designing hospitals? Josh said something about it."

"It's true." Pattie sighed. "I've accepted a position. We're supposed to leave for Connecticut in two more days."

"What are you going to do with your fairyland house?"

Ralph and Pattie looked at each other. "It's for sale."

"Really?" Isa raised her eyebrows.

•   •   •   •   •

The bishop pulled into the parking lot. It had taken him much longer than he expected to get his very tight yellow pants on. In fact, after looking at his bulgy silhouette in the mirror, he was a little grateful it was an "adults-only" party. Jerri drummed her fingers on the dashboard. "Kirt, we are almost half an hour late. I have never been this late to anything in my life."

"I know." He nodded and was reaching out to open his door when his cell phone rang. As he flipped it open, Jerri threw her hands in the air and settled back in her seat with her lips clipped tightly together.

After another few minutes, he put his hand over the mouthpiece. "I'm going to have to deal with this. Sorry."

"Are you kidding?" Jerri nostrils flared.

"It will probably be the last time. I've got to go."

"Fine." She pushed open her door, stood, and slammed it shut. "I can do this." Jerri took a step toward the front door and stopped to adjust her dress. "I can."

•   •   •   •   •

The Jell-O slurping contest was in full swing. Pattie's husband, Ralph, pulled his lips to each side with his index fingers and opened them only slightly, sucking in with all his might to make a wide vacuum cleaner effect. Roy's mouth gaped wide like an angry crow cawing as he breathed in huge mouthfuls of the orange goop, while Kevin was all teeth and tongue, slurping and getting as much inside as out. When the timer buzzed, the difference between the three was almost indistinguishable. The older women from the activities committee hemmed and hawed over the pans for so long that they sucked all the fun out of the experience.

It was in this lull that Jerri made her appearance. Someone yelled, "Oh, my heck!" and a hush fell over the room. For one second she teetered on the edge of self-doubt, but then she sucked it up and stepped forward, smiling. In her best southern drawl, she said, "Yoo-hoo! Cath and Pattie, how do you like my new frock?" For everyone who knew Jerri, this was so out of character that they burst into laughter.

Cath laughed so hard that tears were rolling down her face. She gestured to the open chair beside her, and Jerri came swishing over in her frilly lavender dress with matching shoes. As she got closer, Cath did a double take. Jerri had even put on full makeup. Shockingly, she could have passed for a model in a bridal magazine. She was gorgeous.

"Wow." Cath stared at her friend. "You're breathtaking."

"Da—gum, I'm supposed to look like a nerd." She shook her head and plopped in her seat. "Can't even do that right."

Kevin trotted up to them with green Jell-O from ear to ear. "I won, honey. Can you believe it? Who is your friend?"

"What do you mean?" Cath said. "It's Jerri."

He squinted his eyes. "My goodness, it is."

Jerri laughed. "Well, at least one of us has the nerd thing down."

"Make that two of us." Ralph walked up behind them. "I think we're neck and neck as far as points go."

"Where is your handsome husband? I figured he was our fiercest competition." Kevin looked around.

"He had to go take care of an issue. He's still bishop, remember? Cover your eyebrows because I might get struck by lightning for saying this, but I'm going to be so grateful the day after tomorrow when he's free. Only forty-two hours to go, and I'm counting."

Kevin put a hand on Jerri's shoulder. "Don't worry. I think your feelings are normal. Being bishop is a hard calling, but it's even harder to be the bishop's wife. You have to put up with him being gone and then not even knowing half the time where he is. I can't imagine it. I think you get extra points in heaven for that."

"Well, that's a good thing because I need all the help I can get."

Ralph's gaze darted around the room. "Cath, isn't Hillary on the activities committee?"

"Yes. I'm really surprised she's not here."

Pattie's husband looked back to Jerri and bit his lip. "I'm sure she's doing something important."

⋆　⋆　⋆　⋆　⋆

"Now's the time you've been waiting for," Roy's voice blared from the stage. "Put your lips together and blow—bubblegum, that is."

Jerri was the first to leap to her feet. "I'm all over that. Kevin, are you game?"

"Don't think you're going to leave me in the dust." Ralph hurried behind them.

Cath laughed as they headed toward the stage and then noticed Eden and Josh make their entrance. She had guessed they would take a little extra time getting the children situated and had reserved two chairs at their table next to Isa. She waved, and they came over to sit down. Isa and Pattie had been lost in conversation ever since Ralph went to go slurp Jell-O, but they pulled back from each other as the young couple approached.

"So you are the one I have to thank for this happy reunion?" Pattie jumped up and hugged Eden. "Isa and I are old friends. When I started to conceive of the childcare center, she was the one who told me to never be afraid to reach for my dreams, no matter how big they were."

"That sounds like Isa," Eden said. "Has she told you about her paintings?"

"That's what we've been talking about. I told her the series should be called *Lipstick Wars*, but she won't agree."

Isa held up her hand and shook her head. "Don't think of the name until it's done. It will make itself clear by the end. It always does. Now, I think I heard something about bubblegum, and if I can get in on it, I think I will." Isa leapt to her feet and headed to the stage for the fun.

⋆　⋆　⋆　⋆　⋆

Eden sat next to Josh and looked at the chomping jaws of all of the contestants on stage, trying to soften the huge wads in their mouths. Her eyes were drawn to Marlene, who stood next to her husband. *How dare she judge me so harshly when her children were almost killed by her own neglect? What a hypocrite.*

Eden couldn't sit another second and walked over to the buffet table to get some finger food. She had put a few vegetables and a brownie on her plate when Kimberly and her husband, Brent, walked in. She tried not to look at them and hurried back to her seat, where she covered her face with her hand and began nibbling at the chocolate frosting.

"Hi." Brent's voice was unmistakable, and Eden lifted her eyes enough to meet Kimberly's equal scowl. Brent noticed the interaction with curiosity. "Well, it's good to see you all. I guess we'll sit over there."

Kimberly almost dragged him away, and Eden was happy that her conscience was obviously getting to her. She should feel embarrassed after what she had done.

When Isa returned, she had little flecks of pink stuck to her eyebrows. "I did well, but not as well as Kevin. Does he practice at home?"

Cath shook her head as Kevin made his way back to the table with globs of pink gum embedded all along his hairline. "Wow. This has been an awesome night! I won again!"

"You're not finished yet," Roy's voice boomed from the mike. "All the men who want to participate in the ugly foot contest, come on up. You get double points for this one, and the ladies get to be the judges."

Kevin ran over and grabbed Josh's arm. "You're not getting out of it. Come on."

After a little cajoling, the volunteers had taken off their shoes and stood in a line behind the drawn curtain on the stage with the cuffs of their pants rolled up. Three activities committee members each had a filled pin cushion on their wrists and hurriedly pinned up the thick velvet curtain four inches all along the bottom. The women were then invited up to begin examining the exposed feet.

Cath walked down the row of hairy toes and then stopped and began laughing. One man had on a pair of shoes made of latex that looked like actual feet. They were remarkably lifelike. One of the judges saw them and yelled like a high school referee, "This one is disqualified." She grabbed the wide ankle.

Chuckling, Roy emerged from the stage with the mike still in hand. "You caught me. You caught me. But it's not my fault—for real. Marlene thinks my feet are so ugly, she couldn't let me show 'em to you, as a public service!"

Cath looked at Roy's gnarled hands and thought that Marlene's judgment might have been sound on this one. She continued inspecting the line of bare feet, expecting to recognize her own husband's but found the task to be remarkably difficult. After careful consideration, she had narrowed it down to three.

As the women examined the twenty or so feet, suddenly Isa leaned forward and stared at a younger pair of toes and then ran down about four participants to the left and stared at another. She went over to Eden. "You are not going to believe this. Look at number seven and number twelve really closely."

Eden did and was amazed. As she ran back and forth to check again, she almost bumped into Kimberly. The sight of her whisked away any fun she was having and brought back the gray cloud that had hung over her most of the night. She sat down and folded her arms.

Isa continued spreading the word until Roy asked the contestants to switch places so that the two could stand next to each other.

"I can't believe it! They're foot twins," Cath declared. "How odd. Who are they?"

The curtain parted and out walked Brent and Josh side by side. Cath turned to Eden, who was sitting in a chair beside her. "Can you believe it? You and Kimberly are foot sisters-in-law."

"Great." Eden rolled her eyes and then caught sight of Kimberly staring at her. They peered at each other for a moment until Eden mouthed the words, "How could you?"

With a flick of her black hair, Kimberly marched up to the stage and whispered something to her husband before leaving the room. He quickly put on his shoes and hurried out the door while the judging continued.

The verdict was finally reached. One participant had put green toenail polish on and rather than offend one of the older men with long yellowed nails, it was decided this would be the safest choice. Cath stared at the undisclosed contestant's wiggling toes and wondered if Kevin would go that far, but the feet seemed a little small for him.

No one was more surprised than his wife when Ralph Beckman emerged from behind the stage. Pattie ran up and threw her arms around him. "You did wear a costume after all."

"Of course." He bowed graciously.

⬤   ⬤   ⬤   ⬤   ⬤

At the end of the night, the numbers were tallied up. The group of three old ladies who had spent the night acting as judges chattered away like birds even after handing off the final results. Roy cleared his throat. "Ladies and gentlemen, the numbers have been very close tonight, but one person has taken the cake . . . or should I say the pie? Brother Kevin Reed, would you come to the stage?"

As Kevin made his way to the front, Marlene yanked on Roy's sleeve and whispered something in his ear. He nodded and stood up with a light in his eye. "Now, we had originally discussed having his wife throw the pie, but the ladies over here have a better idea."

Kevin shook his head. "I want Cath to throw it. She's such an awful shot, I won't have to worry about getting messy."

"Well, that may be, but one man in this room was only two points behind you, and these fine ladies think he should get the honor of throwing the pie for being so close to a nerd. What do you think?" Roy's voice boomed, and everyone in the room applauded.

"Oh, no you don't." Kevin looked over Roy's shoulder and covered his mouth in mock fear. "Do you know he's a sharp shooter?"

"Sure do. Brother Ralph Beckman, would you be so kind as to do the honors?" Roy handed Ralph a cream pie, and Kevin obediently sat in the chair at the center of the stage and covered his beloved plaid suit as best he could with the provided plastic table cloth.

Ralph walked slowly in a circle, trying to assess the situation. If he threw it directly at Kevin, it would splatter all over the backdrop of the stage, leaving a terrible mess. There wasn't enough space to get the velocity up by throwing it another direction. He looked at the expectant audience and then made his decision.

He nodded at Roy, who called out, "Ready, set, let her rip!"

Ralph stood four feet in front of Kevin, and, at the signal, threw the pie high in the air and then stepped away. It made a perfect arc and landed squarely on Kevin's head, sloshing down over his face and covering every square inch with white and yellow slush without a single drop touching the curtains. Kevin stuck out his tongue and licked off a little orb around his mouth. "My favorite—banana cream!"

The only one in the room not laughing was Eden.

25
Letting the Weeds Take Over

That night Eden had trouble sleeping. She dreamed that the weeds from the backyard had grown in through the porch windows and crept into the family room. The snakelike branches continued to worm their way through the kitchen cupboards and into her bedroom. When she saw them climbing up her bed, she suddenly remembered the children and ran into their rooms to find that they had been carried up by the curling vines and were high above her head just beyond her reach. She climbed and climbed but couldn't get to them. From her vantage point, she looked down to see the house fall in on itself from the pressure of the weeds until the entire thing was nothing but a small heap of rubble.

Eden woke up shaking and ran down the hall to kiss her toddler and check on the baby. On the way back to her room, she sat in the rocking chair and closed her eyes against the darkness. *How could they have turned against me this way? These women are supposed to be my sisters. They are supposed to be helping me.*

In the quiet she thought she heard an answer, *They are.* All logic told her that wasn't true. The reality was she was totally alone in the world. First, there was her mother who hadn't understood or even tried to help. Then her friends in Primary had abandoned her as soon as her calling was up. And now these women who were her visiting teachers had turned on her. She had no one.

The chill of the night seeped into her bones. Eden sat there shivering for a long time, feeling small and hopeless. At last the first rays of morning began to peek through the window, and she went back to bed.

· · · · ·

The sound of digging woke her up. She wrapped a robe around herself and went to the back door. There was Roy standing next to Brent. Josh was beside Hayden, who sat in the tractor seat with his hands on the steering wheel, having the time of his life.

"Hey, sleepyhead." Josh hurried toward her. "Our good neighbors have agreed to help with the backyard. Can you believe it?"

Her nod was almost imperceptible.

"Roy said the flower beds in the back were so overgrown that we should dig up what plants we want to save and replant them. All that's left is to remove all the debris. When that's done, then he can just mow it all down. If we want to re-establish the flower beds in back later, we can. Is that okay with you? It'll save a lot of time, don't you think?"

Eden nodded again without really listening and went back inside to take a shower. After dressing and feeding Miley, she put the baby in her stroller and walked out the front door.

She couldn't live this way anymore, pretending that everything was all right when it wasn't. Eden decided to head over and talk to Marlene and Kimberly in order to get this whole thing sorted out.

As she turned down the street, she saw Helen Murdock weeding her impeccable front yard. A small green plant from the empty flower bed was pinched between her bony fingers. "They come from your yard, you know," she called out, holding up the tiny intruder.

Eden tried to ignore her, but Helen jogged over and stood right in front of the stroller. "I warned you. I told you to do something about it, and now it's too late." She held up the little plant and shook it in Eden's face. "Years from now, you'll blame me. I know you will, but it is not my fault. It's yours."

"You hateful witch!" Eden yelled. "I'm so sick of your cruel threats and your selfish cold heart that I could scream. No, I am screaming. Why do you hate me so much? Why?"

"It's not about hate, it's about equity," Murdock began.

"Bull! The grossest part of this whole thing is how your hate has seeped into my life and my heart. This isn't worth it. I'd rather live any-where than near you. If you want to purchase the house, you can have it." Eden's chin trembled, but she kept her resolve.

"Oh, no." Helen laughed under her breath. "That offer has been rescinded."

"Really? Why?" Eden read the coldness in Murdock's eyes.

"You'll see soon enough." She walked back toward her trimmed lawn with a perfectly straight back.

Shaken, Eden watched Helen walk away. With the stroller turned the other direction, Eden paused only a minute before abandoning her initial plan and hurrying to the end of the cul-de-sac. She burst through the door as Isa was pouring a warm cup of herbal tea.

Eden collapsed in a kitchen chair and turned the stroller to face her. Miley smiled when she caught her mother's eyes, and Eden couldn't help but give a weak smile in return. She undid the straps, picked up the baby, and then faced Isa. "Tell me what to do. I'm so confused. Helen hates me."

"Helen hates everyone." Isa took a sip of her drink calmly. "Even herself. That's what hate does. When you let it in a little, it grows and grows until it takes over."

"But don't you think some people deserve to be hated? What about your husband?" Eden shot back.

"Charles? Deserve to be hated?" Isa shook her head. "No one deserves to be hated. Hate doesn't destroy the object of that emotion but the carrier of it. Remember my first picture? I hated Charles and what he had done to me, so I tried to cover it up with lipstick, but the hate ate at me. I pushed my children away because they wanted an explanation. I felt their questions were accusations and stopped return-ing their calls."

"The protective wall." Eden thought of her other painting.

"I didn't want others asking questions, so I pushed my friends away too."

"The thorns," Eden remembered.

"If it weren't for you breaking down those walls, I don't know that I'd have seen it. No, I don't hate Charles anymore. I feel sorry for him. I hope he is able to move on, and I hope that I'll be able to grow a new life without him." Isa chuckled to herself and said, "And now the blossoms that are exploding in my life are more beautiful than ever."

Eden bit her lip. "I believe you, but I don't know that I could ever like Helen Murdock."

Isa got up, walked around the table, and sat right beside her friend. "I don't think it's Helen you start with." She sipped her drink again. "I think it's your mother." She raised her eyebrows. Then she stood and walked into the back hall.

Eden shook her head and chased after her, stopping at the entrance of the studio. There was a huge canvas as big as half the back wall. On it was a life-sized picture of her in an empty field. The expression on the face of the girl in the painting was one of sorrow.

"I can still change it, you know." Isa took a sip of her warm drink. "What are you going to choose to do, Eden? You know, we can *choose* to love people who aren't what we want them to be, or at least try. I figure God loves me, and I'm not even close to what he hopes I'll become."

Eden backed up into the hall and silently put Miley in the stroller. This wasn't what she had expected at all. She was the one with the gospel. She was the one who was supposed to teach Isa, wasn't she? She looked up and saw Isa staring at her expectantly.

"I'll think about it," Eden said, stepping out into the cool fall air. "That's the best I can do."

．　　．　　．　　．　　．

Kimberly couldn't believe that Brent was going over to that harpy's house to work on her backyard after all she had told him when they left the party early last night. Eden had promised to keep her pregnancy a secret, and then she told Marlene, of all people. The thought burned in Kimberly's brain, and she wanted to march up there and give that little liar a piece of her mind. Instead, she banged around the house all morning trying to think of things to keep busy.

By noon Kimberly had worked herself up to the point that she was ready for anything. She marched out the front door and up the road to Eden's house. The men were in the backyard—if you could call it that—covered with mud. Although Brent had three new blisters, all the men looked exhausted, and the pickup was filled to the brim with rusted junk, it still looked like nothing more than an overgrown field.

Worst of all, Eden wasn't anywhere to be seen.

Kimberly was in knots. She had all this emotion and nowhere to dump it. As she turned to go, a solution presented itself. Not two steps down the street she came face to face with Marlene. "I've got some things I need to set straight," Kimberly began, pointing her finger in Marlene's face.

"Yes?" Marlene answered simply.

Kimberly took a deep breath and decided to catch Marlene with her own words. "First, tell me one thing. When did you talk to Eden about me?"

"Eden? I haven't spoken to her for a while."

Kimberly stomped her foot without thinking. "Then how did you find out about my pregnancy?"

"Cath said she heard that you and Eden had seen each other at the doctor's office. She brought over the gift," Marlene explained.

Kimberly stood there dumbfounded. *So Cath knows too? Who hadn't that little gossip told?*

26

Lingering Morning Kisses

It was Sunday morning, and they had to be out the door by six thirty to meet with the stake president. Cath got ready with ten minutes to spare before they had to leave, knowing how important it was to Kevin that he was on time. As she tiptoed into Sandra's room to give her final instructions on getting the roast in the oven, Cath looked around at this extension of her daughter's life. She noticed the row of trophies and ribbons from her years on the track team and her desk piled high with books from her AP classes this year.

Cath winced at the pile of clean clothes still unfolded in the basket on the floor but had to admire that her daughter had washed the load herself. On the nightstand the scriptures lay open, and Cath's heart overflowed with pride at all her beautiful daughter was becoming. Without even thinking, she bent down and kissed a sleeping Sandra on the forehead, leaving a bright lipstick mark.

"I love you," Cath whispered.

"Yeah, Mom," her daughter mumbled with her eyes still closed. "I promise I'll get dinner in, and I know that Kimberly and Brent are going to come and drive the minivan to church, so we'll have a ride." She yawned and rolled over. "I'll be there after all, so don't worry."

Cath smiled, thinking of how surprised Sandra would be when she discovered the lipstick kiss on her forehead. It gave her an idea. One by one she went to each of the boys' rooms and planted a kiss on their cheeks or nose. When they woke up and looked in the mirror, she could imagine that each would know of their mother's love, even while they slept. She rushed to the already warmed car. Kevin looked at her suspiciously. "What did you do?"

"Who, me?" Cath raised her eyebrows and opened her eyes wide.

"I'm sure I'll find out before the day is over." He put the car into gear and headed toward the chapel.

• • • • •

Scrubbing her bottom teeth one last time, Kimberly spit in the sink and looked at her worn face. She had played the scene over and over in her mind all night and still didn't know what to make of it. When Cath called and asked them to drive her family to church, Kimberly had almost brought it up then, but the words wouldn't come.

If she really had faith in the blessing she was given, why was she so upset that people knew about the baby? As her emotions began to cool down, other things became clearer. Marlene had approached Kimberly right after her talk with Eden, so the timing was off. Eden would have had to talk to Cath long before they spoke, and chances were Eden didn't even remember doing it.

Kimberly was embarrassed by her behavior and knew the outburst was based on fear. But how could she overcome it? She walked over to her bed and reached down to grab her scriptures. The words from John came to her mind, something about perfect love casting out fear. But whose love and how could she feel it? Frustrated and confused, she hurried to the car where her husband was waiting.

• • • • •

Eden sat on the last row before the back aisle. They had arrived ten minutes early, but it was the only place left besides the breezeway, which opened to the gym and the stage. She knew if they sat back there, Hayden would eventually find a way to run around on the wooden floor and disturb the entire meeting. Josh and Eden had opted for squeezing in next to an elderly couple with the children on both their laps.

The only other space in the crowded chapel was on the third row. The bishop's wife sat alone, holding about half the row empty despite a number of people determined to steal it from her.

"So what's your guess about the next bishop?" Josh whispered above the roar of the conversations around them.

"I have no idea. They'll probably call one of the counselors." Eden adjusted the baby on her lap and looked around the room, trying to catch sight of Kimberly or Hillary, neither of whom appeared to be present.

Suddenly the room grew quiet, exposing the soft prelude that Cath was playing on the organ. The man next to Eden was chuckling under his breath, and she flipped her head toward the aisle to see why and covered her mouth.

Sandra and her brothers were walking forward with their arms folded, each sporting a bright lipstick kiss. Sandra's was on her forehead, while Jordan had a simple kiss mark on his cheek. Ten-year old Carson's was smack dab on the end of his nose. But it was Mike who stole the show.

Laughter peeled through the chapel as little Mike smiled a toothy grin punctuated on either side by the traces of two round puckers. The color looked suspiciously like the one his mother was wearing, and she gave a wink to them from her place behind the keyboard.

Eden's shoulders began to shake silently as she realized the depth of love that family had for each other. How grateful she was for Cath's friendship. She watched as the children passed by and then let in a sharp breath. Kimberly and her husband were walking behind them. It seemed like Kimberly was trying to smile in her direction, but Eden turned her head away in disgust.

The opening of the meeting was a blur until after the sacrament when the stake president stood to make the big announcement. "We're grateful for the loving service of Bishop Miller. He'll be sorely missed. I have to say that as we were praying about who should be called in his stead, I've never had a more clear answer—even after his performance at the ward party the other night." The congregation laughed and then quickly settled down, waiting for the final word. "We'd like to call Kevin Reed as your next bishop."

Eden sat stunned for a moment. She stood with the baby, wiggled past her husband and Hayden, and rushed from the room with Miley sleeping on her shoulder.

She sat undisturbed in the nursing mother's lounge for the next two hours, trying not to think about what the call would mean. It had been so wonderful to have someone help her with the children and be there for her. But now Cath would be so busy she wouldn't have time for anyone or anything else, and Eden already knew how that felt.

At least she could be there for Sandra. Maybe there was a purpose in their friendship, and it would all work out. As the second hour wore on, Eden continually looked toward the door. *What's taking Sandra so long?* Miley's diaper was so soggy it puffed between her legs, but Eden had forgotten the diaper bag and didn't dare leave with the swirling hurricane of emotions welling inside her.

At the buzz of the second bell, she finally stepped in the hall to see Sandra, surrounded by a group of teens her age, involved in active conversation. Eden squared her shoulders, patted the baby in the crux of her arm, and marched down the hall toward the Relief Society Room until she heard her name. Stopping, she held her mouth firm.

"I'm so glad I caught you, Eden, I mean, Sister Duncan." Sandra touched her arm.

"What can I do for you?" Eden tried to sound mature and nonchalant.

"I wanted you to know . . . well . . ." Sandra lowered her eyes and searched for the words. "I'm going to start going to Sunday School every week, and I'm going to be on time to seminary."

"Why, because your dad was called as bishop?" The words shot from Eden's mouth, filled with hurt, but she didn't care.

"No, I didn't even know about my dad being bishop when I made the decision." Sandra tucked a tight blonde curl behind her ear. "It started the morning after the nerd party. You saw Dad's suit, right?" She raised her eyebrows and smiled at Eden.

"It was ugly," Eden admitted.

"Well, when Mom got it out, she found this old seventies song about the Book of Mormon, and the next morning she had an emergency family home evening to teach it to us. The thing was totally cheesy with little tinkling cymbals in the background and everything. Chin-ga, chin-ga, chin-ga, chin." She imitated the sound and closed her eyes.

"Really." Eden moved the baby to her other side, wondering where this was headed.

"But the message was actually cool. Mom had me read the scripture, you know that one the missionaries always use about praying about the Book of Mormon and everything. Do you know what the next line says?"

Eden shook her head.

"It says that by the Holy Ghost you can know the truth of all things." She lifted her eyebrows. "Remember what we talked about the other night? About only acting on things you really know?"

Eden swallowed and looked down. "Yes," she whispered.

"Well, when you left, I was so screwed up. I had totally convinced myself that I didn't know the gospel was true. I mean, I felt it and everything, but I didn't know for sure, so I thought it'd be better not to go to church."

"What?" Eden looked alarmed.

"I know. It was stupid, huh? I really did know the whole time, just like I knew about Cory. The Spirit had been telling me, but I wasn't listening."

"I'm so sorry."

Sandra leaned in closer and put out a finger. Little Miley clutched at it, and she smiled at the baby. "Ya know, when I told my Mom about Zee's brother, she had me call the bishop right away." Sandra looked both ways and then said in a hushed voice, "I'm not supposed to share this with everyone, but Cory's dad was removed from their home by the police last night. Isn't that great? He's safe now. See, I knew it. I knew it."

"I'm sorry I didn't believe you." Eden's face reddened.

"What do you mean? The problem was that I didn't believe myself, and then I realized why. You can only know for sure if you have the Spirit, right?" She twirled her finger in the air in a circular motion, expecting Eden to make the connection herself.

"And?" Eden shook her head, clueless.

"Well, duh? I've been skipping Sunday School and getting to seminary as late as I possibly could. What's up with that?" She laughed at herself. "So that's when I decided I'm going to be a hundred-percenter from now on. Well, I better head off to Young Women. Call me if you need someone to watch your kids."

Sandra was halfway up the hall by the time she finished her last word and ducked in the doorway to Young Women. Eden stood in the empty hall alone, the words echoing in her mind. *Because of something I said, Sandra had almost decided never to come back to church.* Eden covered her mouth with her hand, unsure of what to do. Then she heard the door to her right open and watched Hayden back into the hall.

"Don't even think it." Eden's voice was stern.

Hayden stared at his mom a second with his hand still on the knob and stepped back in the nursery.

27

Evidence of Love

Isa's head jerked in the direction of the "for sale" sign in the front yard. She sprinted to the porch and punched the buzzer over and over again in rapid succession, hoping they hadn't left for church already. At last the door opened to Pattie's husband.

"I'm sorry it's so early, but I tried to call a dozen times yesterday and at least that many this morning." Isa took a few deep breaths, trying to calm herself as Pattie approached them.

"Sorry." Ralph raised his hand with a sudden smile. "That was my fault. I packed up all the phones yesterday."

"Are they still here?" Isa rushed through the front door and stood by the mauve dining room wall with a hand over her chest. A silhouette of a child reading a book in a rich burgundy brought her peace. "I talked to your Realtor, who said you were going to paint over everything. I couldn't believe my ears."

"She thought it would sell better," Pattie answered weakly.

"Well, she's a heartless dolt. That's what I say." Isa stepped over to the other wall and smiled at the picture of the little girl chasing a butterfly. "Do you remember when I wanted to make the butterfly have color, and you wouldn't let me?" Isa laughed.

"Do I ever." Pattie smiled at the thought. "You never had my vision of the place."

"Maybe not, but I always had your love of it." Isa strolled over to the back window where the garden's fierce colors seem to vibrate through the whole house.

"That you did." Pattie nodded.

"So if I were to purchase this home, would you be upset if I finally let that poor butterfly have its wings?"

"But I thought you already had a place." Pattie looked to her husband in disbelief.

"I'm living in a garage," Isa said blandly.

"I couldn't think of anything I'd like better." Pattie threw her arms around her and hugged her with all her might.

By the time they got the details clarified and had waved good-bye to Isa, sacrament meeting was over. Pattie sat on the bare sofa. "I'm sorry we missed it. Who do you think they called as bishop?"

Ralph slid his jacket over his shoulders. "What do you mean we missed it? We'll only be forty-five percent late, if you count all three hours."

"I suppose you're right." Pattie stood. "But you are the only person I know who defines lateness by percentage points."

28

Facing Issues

Eden was about to step into the Relief Society room when someone grabbed her arm. Hillary stared at her huffing. "Wait right there."

She ran over to the library window, and after some cross words, Sister Witherby closed the door and headed to the nursery, glaring at Hillary the entire time. Once the door was shut, Hillary grabbed Eden's free arm and guided her out the back exit to the empty sidewalk at the rear of the building. "It was you, wasn't it?"

"What are you talking about?" Eden patted Miley, who was making little moaning noises, reacting to the tension and her drenched diaper.

"Oh, I figured it out." Hillary folded her arms and tucked her chin toward her chest. "You thought I gave you a bad review, and so you told them about my husband and Cory to get me back. Well, I didn't do it. I said just what you wanted me to. It was Marlene who was nearly mute and that tall, mean neighbor who tore you apart."

"Kimberly." Eden said under her breath.

Hillary lifted her hands as if to strike out but simply shook them in the air. "Don't try to change the subject. Because of you, Cory won't have a dad. How are we supposed to live and pay rent? You ruined everything."

"Cory's your son?" Eden had never put it together. Hillary glared at her, and Eden shook her head. "No, I promise. I knew nothing about this, and if I had, I would have come to you first."

With her hands on her hips, Hillary stared at her without saying a word for at least three long minutes. "Well, all right, then. I'll let it go—this time." She turned and marched back through the door, leaving Eden alone.

Too shocked to go back inside, Eden decided to walk around the building. The afternoon was warm, and her thoughts were all jumbled into knots in her brain. As she stepped down the single stair to the sidewalk, Eden noticed something dart out the side door far across the lawn at the other corner of the building. A car screeched its tires, and her heart jumped.

Clutching Miley, she sprinted across the yard. A crowd had gathered, and Eden pushed her way through the people until she came to Ralph Beckman on his knees, hovering over a little boy. All she could see were the child's shoes—Hayden's shoes. She held Miley close to her and fell to her knees.

Ralph moved back, and a little tear-stained face looked up at her.

"I don't think he was hit—just scared." He moved back beside his shaking wife and put an arm around her. "We both were."

Relief flooded through Eden's entire body as she knelt beside her son. "Can you stand up?" she asked him.

Hayden threw his arms around her and clamped on tight as Ralph turned and began to encourage the small crowd to disperse. Eden knelt there, taking in deep gulps of air and hugging her little boy with one hand while cradling her infant in the other until her heart rate returned to normal. The baby began to squirm, and, with effort, she hefted both children up. "Come on, buddy, let's go find Dad."

Determined to leave as soon as possible, Eden made her way through the door and down the hall. This incident would be one more thing Hillary would use against her. She could imagine how Hillary would spin the events to make the whole thing her fault. And Kimberly, she never wanted to see her again. *I thought she was my friend and that I could trust her.*

Eden clamped her arm more tightly around Hayden's legs and adjusted how she held him. As she walked down the hall, the Savior's words came to her mind. *Love your enemies. Do good to them who curse you. Pray for those who despitefully use you.*

She passed the bishop's office, entered the foyer, and had barely sat down in the orange upholstered chair when Josh stepped out from the hall she had just been in. He hurried over to her and knelt. "Are you all right? You look like you've seen a ghost."

"Almost." Eden touched Hayden's face, and he snuggled closer to her. "I'll tell you about it later. Are you ready to go? Because I sure am."

"I've got to return this to the library." He got to his feet and ran up the other hall. In a little bit, Josh came jogging back. "Wow, do I have news for you." He walked up and took Miley and then looked around. "Where's the diaper bag and baby carrier?"

"I guess they're still in the chapel. Didn't you take them with you?" She gently pried the still frightened Hayden away from her neck and passed him to her husband. "I'll get them. Why don't you start loading the children in the car?"

Eden stuck her head in the chapel and saw Cath surrounded by her friends over by the organ. Even from that distance, she could tell Pattie was shaking from the incident outside and guessed they were talking about it. Feeling like she had no choice, Eden entered the chapel, holding her breath and hoping she would not be seen. She snuck up to the last pew.

"Oh, Eden, I'm so sorry. Is Hayden all right?" In no time Cath was running up the aisle.

The sudden show of sympathy was too much for her, and Eden blinked back tears. "He's great, okay. I've got to go." She grabbed her stuff and hurried into the foyer before Cath could catch her. With her arms full, she turned around backwards to hit the pushbar on the front door with her lower back as Kimberly appeared from around the corner.

"There you are. I've been looking for you all day." Kimberly rushed to her side.

Eden stopped cold halfway out the door and took a deep breath. From the direction she'd come from, Eden guessed that Kimberly must have been talking to the new bishop too. She turned to look at her and thought about Hillary's description. *Tall and mean.*

Kimberly came right up to her and whispered. "I'm so sorry. I jumped to conclusions that weren't right—" She watched Eden's face and bit her thumbnail. Then she dropped her hand and repeated. "I'm so sorry."

Eden glared at her. "You should be! I don't think I can look at you, let alone talk to you." Eden stomped out the door and ran to her car.

29

Breaking Down the Wall

Eden spent another restless night. Her mind wouldn't slow down. In her dream she walked out the front door and noticed that the flowers the men had transplanted were growing. The wonderful smell and bright colors made her smile, and she invited the blossoms into her door.

The plants grew across the carpet, blooming in bright bursts of color. They surrounded the doorways and window sills, covering up all the cracks and holes that had worried her. She watched as Hayden and Miley played in the soft garden around them. Outside Eden could see the last of the peeling blue paint covered by an explosion of flowering plants until every bit of her life was filled with beauty.

Afterward, she lay in bed awake for nearly an hour, thinking about it. That was the thing she wanted for her life, but how could she begin? *If I could only talk to someone. I can't call Cath after being so rude at church, and Isa tried to help me, but I wouldn't listen.*

The rhythmic sound of her husband's deep breathing annoyed her, and she jostled him lightly so that if he did wake up, he wouldn't think it was intentional. He rolled over, smacking his lips together three times before drifting back into his comatose state.

It was five thirty in the morning when Eden got out of bed and headed to the kitchen. The answer was obvious. Isa had told her about it days ago. She knew she couldn't wait another minute, so she picked up the phone and dialed. It took a little longer than normal, but after the fourth ring, her mother answered, "Hope Lane. I'm here for you."

"It's Eden."

"Is everything all right?" Her mom asked with a hoarse voice, still tinged with sleep.

"Mom, I miss you."

•　•　•　•　•

Fran, the city secretary, balanced her cup of coffee on top of the four files she had been reviewing at home during the weekend and sat deftly in her chair. Monday mornings were always a pain, and this week was even worse with the town meeting coming up on Friday afternoon. When the phone rang, she waited before answering it, hoping it had already clicked over to the machine, but she picked it up one ring early without thinking. The voice on the line was loud and curt.

"I am calling on behalf of Family Protective Services. We are currently investigating a case and received a report that a home was condemned with children living on the premises."

"What's the address?" Fran had dealt with such calls on a regular basis and was not surprised. There were two problem areas in town—an abandoned apartment complex and a half-completed building project. If the cost of demolition wasn't prohibitive, they would have been long gone. The city had even recently passed a resolution allowing neighbors to pay for demolition of condemned properties, but no one had stepped forward to foot the bill. She took down the address and scooted her black leather business chair across the small office to the file cabinet.

As Fran put her hands on the file and lifted it, her mouth dropped open. *This has to be a mistake.* She stood and ran back to the phone. "I've never seen this before. I've got to check into it," she stammered.

"Could you simply tell me if the document is there?" asked the snippy voice on the phone.

"It's here, but I don't think the owner has ever been notified properly. I . . ."

"So the home is condemned, and can you confirm children are living on the premises?"

"Yes, I believe that is the case."

"Please forward copies of the condemnation order to this address. I'll need to verify your personal information."

"Yes, of course." The words washed over her as Fran finished the conversation and hung up the phone. The house had been vacant for years, and the owner had been reticent in answering their calls. Fran had remembered talking about having the house condemned, but then it had quickly gone up for sale. *Without proper notification it couldn't be legally binding, could it?* she wondered.

A sly smile suddenly played across Fran's face as she realized the opportunity in front of her. Fran grabbed the file and marched to her desk. This was a serious mistake. It could cause issues with the state and even turn into a civil suit, and she had a pretty good idea who sat at the center of the whole thing. Fran laughed to herself, pulled up a new window on her computer, and added another item to the agenda.

Satisfied, she picked up the phone and dialed. "Marlene?"

. . . . .

Tuesday morning brought frigid temperatures and cloudy skies. The drafty house could not stay warm enough, and Eden had gotten up in the middle of the night to put the children in thick flannel sleepers. She had donned woolen camping socks and wore a thick hooded jersey over her nightgown while Josh, aka Mr. Freeze, seemed unaffected. He emerged fresh from the shower and sat down to the eggs and toast she put in front of him.

"Can I ask you a favor?" he said, smiling.

"Anything."

"I filled out a few resumes online last night and need these applications mailed." He slid the envelopes across the table.

"You've really decided to leave your job?" she asked.

"If I can find something else," Josh answered. "Nothing is worth this. I don't know when I'll be home." He shoved two bites of egg in his mouth and grabbed his jacket. "I love you."

Eden nodded, looked at the letters, and covered her face. She had been so self-consumed that she hadn't even noticed how hard things had been for him. She heard his car pull away and put his plate in the sink as the phone rang.

"I know what you're doing this afternoon." Her mother sounded breathless with excitement.

"What are you talking about, Mom?"

"Our vacation—I have a new listing for this cute little rustic cabin by a lake. It's only forty-five minutes away with no phone or cell service. I've got an open window of time this morning and would love for you to go with me to check it out."

Eden knew her mother was really trying harder to be sweet, and she appreciated it, but she still didn't understand anything about her. "Mom, do you remember I have a new baby? I don't think there's any way I can make it."

"Of course you can. Just call someone. I've got to be back by two thirty and have a ten o'clock meeting this morning. That gives you thirty five minutes to pull it together. Make it work, Eden."

Muffled cries came from down the hall. "Mom, I've got to go. The baby's awake."

"Call me." The phone clicked, and there was silence on the line.

Eden hurried to get the baby, knowing there was no one she could call.

30

The Very Edge

By mid-morning Miley was kicking happily on a blanket in the middle of the floor while Hayden played with his trucks. The phone rang, and Eden tried to think of what excuse she would give to her mother.

"Hey, girl, it's almost the end of the month, and I was calling about visiting teaching. Do you still want that change?" The Relief Society president's voice was a welcome surprise.

"I'm not sure what I want," Eden admitted. "Do what you think is best." They chatted for a few more minutes, and as she hung up, Eden felt a little guilty. The truth was she hadn't been that great a visiting teacher to Cath or Marlene. With the phone still in her hand, she dialed Cath's number and let it ring twice, but she heard a knock on the door and went to answer it.

There, standing before her, was Cath with a plate of cowboy cookies. Eden threw open the door. "What a nice surprise."

"What kind of a visiting teacher would I be if I didn't do an emergency visit at the end of the month?" She laughed.

"I don't know, but you must be inspired because I was just thinking about you."

"Did Brenda call you, too?" Cath asked through hooded eyes.

"Yup, I guess we were both inspired by her. Come on in." When Hayden saw Cath, he jumped to his feet and ran over to her. She hugged him and handed him the plate of cookies to take to the kitchen, which he did proudly. Miley was living up to her name, giggling at the play gym hanging over her on the floor when the phone rang again. Eden ran to answer it.

Her mother was on the line. "So, did you get someone to watch the kids?"

"Mom, I can't leave them for the entire afternoon."

"Yes, you can," Cath called from the other room. She was sitting on the ground playing with Miley. "I don't have to be home until 3:25. Will that be enough time?"

"Okay, it looks like I can, Mom." She could hardly believe the words as they left her mouth. "I'll be there in half an hour." Eden hung up and walked over to Cath, who was consumed in reading a book to Hayden. "Are you sure about this? Miley has just started to take a bottle."

Cath patted Eden on the arm. "It's the least I can do. I am your visiting teacher, after all. Well, have a great time."

"I'll try." Eden ran from the room and threw on jeans and a T-shirt. She pulled back her hair and looked at her naked face in the mirror. She started to reach below the sink for her makeup bag but stopped herself, deciding instead to run out the door as she was.

•   •   •   •   •

A few minutes later, Cath heard a knock at the door and got up, assuming Eden had forgotten something. "Roy? How can I help you?"

"I had a free morning and decided to work on the back forty there. Do you think Eden will mind?"

Cath smiled. "I think she'll be thrilled. Go right ahead."

•   •   •   •   •

The tires made a crunching sound against the gravel driveway, and Eden sat back and closed her eyes. Her mom had spent the majority of the ride on her cell phone, but it had allowed her time to think, for which she was grateful.

For some reason, Isa's words kept coming back to her. All the anger she felt at being betrayed by Kimberly and Hillary didn't seem worth it. She had to forgive them, not as a gift to them, but as a gift to herself so she wouldn't be filled with this grayness inside of her. She looked over at her mother and felt the same thing. She had to accept that her mom didn't have the same views she did, but she could still love her. She had to.

The car turned the corner onto a thin dirt road surrounded by greenery. There were no signs of civilization anywhere, and the tires kicked up a layer of fine dust that seeped through the smallest cracks.

"Wow." Eden tried to peer through the blackberries and ferns. "It looks like we've driven right to the very edge of humanity."

"You mean to the edge of my sanity." Her mother secured the cell into its stand on the dash and gave a harsh laugh. There was a sharp dip in the road followed by a tight turn, and then her mom abruptly slammed on the brakes.

A large A-frame nestled in a grove of majestic pines sat directly in front of them. About twenty yards off to the right, mist rose from the amber depths of a crystalline lake. The smooth green lawn faded into the shore where two weather worn canoes sat belly-up like well-fed sea lions next to a freshly painted white deck.

Her mom clicked her tongue in disgust. "This will never do. He did not tell me it was one of those seventies monstrosities."

Eden took in the lush lawn with fresh mums still in full bloom bordering the front deck and the gleaming windows shining in the morning sun. "Mom, give it a chance. Maybe it will be nice inside."

"Just looking at it makes me want to don puka shells. I can't believe they didn't tell me it was an A-frame." She slid the car into park and cut the engine. "I mean, honestly, who cares what the inside is like if the outside is hideous."

"I do," Eden said.

"Well, you would."

"What is that supposed to mean?"

Her mom looked at her intently. "Let's be honest. You were so cute in high school, and now you're letting yourself go. Are you even wearing makeup today?"

"As a matter of fact, I'm not because I thought it would only be the two of us, so it wouldn't matter." Eden leaned back in her seat.

"Well, how do you like that? I don't matter." Her mom grinned at the way she had turned her daughter's words around and grabbed the door handle to leave the car.

"No, Mom, you're the only one that matters to you. You're all you think about. I never matter. My husband doesn't matter. My children don't matter." The words spilled out of Eden's mouth unchecked before she could stop herself. "Mom, do you realize that you've never gotten Josh's name right? I've been married to him for almost five years." She was breathing hard and turned in her seat with pleading eyes.

Hope Lane's face turned to stone. "You don't want to go there with me, Eden."

"Mom, I had Miley over two months ago, and you've never even seen her. You've never set eyes on her beautiful face. You're her grandmother, and you don't even know what she looks like. What's up with that?"

"I'm your mother, and I have to love you, but I don't need to take responsibility for your mistakes."

"Mistake? You think Miley is a mistake? She's not. We wanted her. We love her." She turned slowly to face her mother. "Aren't I a mistake, too?"

Her mom didn't answer. The silence was shattered by the sharp ring of the cell phone. "Hope Lane. I'm here for you." Eden watched her mother straighten up, slap a plastic smile on her face, start up the car, and put it in reverse. After a few minutes, she turned to her daughter as if nothing had been said. "This call is important. I've got to get back to the city right away. We'll do this some other time."

Her mother managed to stay on the phone the entire way back to town, and Eden watched as the world whizzed by, feeling detached and unsure if she could ever fix anything. Finally, they pulled up next to her car. Eden got out in front of her mom's office and was about to close the car door when her mom put down the phone.

"Stop." Hope tightened her lips together and closed her eyes.

"Mom," Eden pleaded. "I wanted to—"

"Don't say anything." Her mother almost screamed but then added softly, "Just listen. I have spent my whole life trying to please you, and it's never been good enough. I was a single mom and didn't want you to grow up in some cruddy apartment, so I worked hard FOR YOU, but you always seemed mad at me. It was never enough."

Eden shook her head, "No, I—"

Hope raised her hands. "Just listen." She took a deep breath and continued. "When that family moved in across the street, it was worse. I was suddenly evil, and when they left, you told me over and over how you wanted a sister. I was single. How could I do that?"

"I was a kid. I didn't know," Eden whispered.

"So I've been weird since you've had this new baby, but don't you get it? Hayden finally has a sister. You did something for him I couldn't. You won." She swallowed and looked away.

"Mom, it's not like that."

She turned back to her daughter. "All I ever wanted was for you to love me, really love me. But I've never been good enough for you." The phone rang, and Hope checked the caller ID. "I've got to take this. We'll talk later."

She reached over, pulled the door closed, and sped away. Eden watched her leave and shoved an errant tear off her cheek.

* * * * *

It wasn't even noon yet as Eden drove up her street. She gripped the steering wheel so tightly that her knuckles were white. Isa didn't have a clue how hard this was. *How can I love a mother who only cares for me out of obligation and considers my sweet baby a mistake?* The idea felt like a wildfire burning through her brain, devouring every other thought.

Halfway up her street, Eden noticed a husband helping his wife out of the car. She realized she was speeding and hit the brakes, staring intently at the couple who she suddenly recognized as Kimberly and Brent. Kimberly was walking slightly bent over like an old lady with Brent supporting most of her weight. For a split second Eden and Kimberly's eyes caught, and in that moment, Eden recognized the hollow agony of grief.

31

A Silent Whisper

Cath couldn't believe it when she heard the car drive up out front. It hadn't even been two hours. She was rocking the baby, who was hovering on the verge of sleep, while Hayden put together a puzzle for the eighth time on the floor at her feet. Everything seemed so right, and Cath felt her heart stir. *Someone's waiting for you.*

She flipped her head around. The voice was so clear. But it didn't come from the outside; it came from somewhere deep within her. She wanted to pretend that she had imagined it, but the thought seemed a sacrilege. *My husband was just made bishop. How could I have another baby? It's ridiculous.*

In response, warmth filled her, and her eyes edged with tears. In that moment the front door swept open, and there stood Eden. "So how did it go?"

Hayden jumped up and ran to his mom. Cath avoided eye contact and stood with the baby. The jostling woke Miley, and she began to cry.

Eden took her little one, and immediately the infant cuddled up against her mother's neck, recognizing her.

The scene again awoke something inside of Cath that her independent heart did not want to succumb to. She blinked away any evidence of her feelings and turned to pick up the puzzle on the floor. "Everything went fine. You're back early," Cath said, hoping to divert her mind with conversation.

"Yeah, well, it seems my mom wasn't as available as she thought." Eden sat in the rocking chair.

"I understand." Cath put the puzzle on top of the bookshelf and turned.

"Are you all right?" Eden asked, peering at Cath's flushed face.

"Yeah, I've got some things on my mind." Cath's voice sounded strained, as if she was trying to hold back her tears. "I've got to go now. Call me if you need anything." Cath grabbed her purse and ran out the door, shutting it behind her.

• • • • •

Once in the driver's seat, Cath sat for a few minutes before turning the key. In her mind she could see a little baby girl with jet black hair and icy blue eyes lying far away. Between them lay a long path covered with burning hot coals. She looked down at her bare feet and wiggled her naked toes. *Would you do it?*

Opening her eyes, Cath turned on the car, but the question kept pounding in her brain. *Would I do it? Would I cross that painful path for that child?*

She thought about all that she would do for each of her children. How she would go through any trial, face any struggle, any sacrifice. Without question, she'd give all she had for any one of them. The thought of burnt feet made her laugh. *Of course I would, without hesitating,* she thought.

So why am I hesitating now?

Peace filled her until one more thought came to her mind, which made her start to sweat. *How do I tell Kevin?*

32

A Little Bit of Eden

Within minutes of being nursed, Miley was asleep in her crib. Hayden had zonked out on the floor at the same time. Eden got up and started a load of wash in the garage. *Man, Cath seemed upset when she left. She's probably had her fill of babysitting.* Eden tried to shrug off the guilt that overwhelmed her, but she couldn't. *How could Mom blame me for her own issues?* "It's not my fault." Her words echoed against the cold walls.

Amid everything she was coping with, something else seemed to be fighting for her attention. It was that look in Kimberly's eyes as Eden drove past minutes before. It haunted her and took priority. *Be realistic. The last person Kimberly would want to see at a time like this is me.* Her last words to Kimberly at church had been so cruel. *It's like Isa said, I've pushed everyone away, and now I'm alone.*

Eden turned and hurried back to the living room. Hayden had awakened and was trying to shove Spiderman into his Fisher-Price airplane. He was getting more frustrated by the minute and began pounding the toys against each other. Eden remembered Cath's clever way of dealing with the toy basket by employing distraction and paused. Then she walked to the front door without a word and opened it. With her hand held out she said, "Hey, buddy, let's go play."

Eden was quite certain she'd be able to hear the baby through the thin single-paned windows if they stayed close to the house. Besides, she needed fresh air to think. They stepped off the rotting front porch and turned to notice the vivid flowers of white, orange, purple, and maroon that dappled the smooth flower bed from her husband's Saturday efforts.

The bright yellow buttons at the center of the purple asters looked like velvet, and Hayden bent down and touched one. Eden noticed the soil around them was dark, and her forehead furrowed. Someone had watered them recently. Curious, she clutched her son's hand and headed around the back corner of the house. Mother and son stood paralyzed at the sight. The backyard was completely transformed. They stepped reverently up to the gate. What had been a tangled mess of briars and weeds was now the loveliest lawn she had ever seen.

The rusted latch did not want to give but succumbed on the second tug, and the two entered hand in hand, mother and child, both in awe. The little grove of trees at the back of the property had always been unreachable due to the overgrowth. Now she could see bright apples and plump yellow pears almost ready to be picked. The old gnarled trees were gorgeous with wide low branches that screamed for her to climb them. She resisted but could imagine Josh up on the branch overhead with his feet dangling and Hayden on his lap.

She twirled around and noticed the broad stretch of green lawn between the trees and house with plenty of room to run and play. A quaint stone walkway that had been entirely hidden under the old weeds curled behind them. There was even a cast iron bench beside a small pile of stones that may have once been a small fish pond. She sat on the ancient bench while Hayden squatted and explored each rock, piling the best ones off to the side, busy and proud of his accomplishment.

Eden looked on and couldn't help but smile, even after all the horrific things that had happened that morning.

Who could have done this? she wondered for a split second and then had to admit it was Roy and probably Brent helping. *Brent*, she thought and was suddenly flooded with guilt. She couldn't imagine what he and his wife were going through. It was so clear now that Kimberly's anger was simply fear in disguise—and for good reason. The thought of Eden's own angry words stung again. But she couldn't go over there. It would be an invasion of Kimberly's privacy. *After all, I'm the last person she'd want to see.*

Eden thought about calling the Relief Society president, but if sharing news about the pregnancy upset Kimberly, it might be even worse to tell someone about her losing the baby. She didn't know what to do and was relieved to hear the distant cry of her baby through the window. "Come on, Hayden. Let's get your sister. She might like playing out here too."

* * * * *

Flora hurried to her desk after most of her morning had been wasted in a staff meeting. She picked up the phone and began dialing. "Sergeant Murphy? Flora from Family Services here. I've got a citation that needs to be delivered. I'll fax you the details. When do you think you can have it served?"

"Well, darlin', you've caught me at a good time. I had a cancellation this afternoon, so I can have it out in the next half hour if you get it to me right away."

"Done." She hit *send* on her computer screen, wrote a few hand-scribbled notes on the inside flap of the folder, and closed it. Twisting around, she stood and marched across the room, dumping the file in a wire basket on the counter labeled "Child Intervention."

She strolled back to her seat, pleased with herself. This was the fourth case she had completed that morning. For the first time in a long time, Flora was finally feeling like she was at least treading water instead of drowning under an impossible workload.

When she returned to her desk, her face fell. Six new folders had been stuck in her inbox.

33

Finding Motherhood

The afternoon should have been magical. Both children were filled with giggles, and Eden found an old rope swing that was still intact. The weathered hemp stretched to the point where the soft wood seat was less than a foot off the ground, perfect for Hayden, who switched back and forth from flying on his stomach like Superman to straddling the seat while holding onto one side like he was riding a horse.

Eden laid out a large quilt and watched as Miley curled her back and rolled over for the first time. The autumn afternoon air was warm with a clean crisp edge, but behind it all one thing plagued her. She knew she had to visit Kimberly. *What could I do besides upset her? Kimberly wouldn't even want to see me.*

By the middle of the afternoon, Eden knew she could no longer ignore the definite prompting and took the children inside. Hayden was worn out. She set him in front of the TV with a Disney movie and put the baby in her swing. In the closet she kept the expensive gift bags her mother gave her every birthday and Christmas, usually filled with toiletry items. Eden found a simple one made from earthy brown paper and grabbed some crumpled white tissue. On the mantel she had a little figurine that she had bought right after she was married. It was an angel with a dove in her hand.

Eden wrapped the figurine in the tissue and put it in the bag. She closed her eyes and said a simple prayer. When she lifted her head, she chided herself for how silly she was being. There was no way she could go to Kimberly's. Bringing the children would be like pouring salt in an open wound, and there was no way she could ask Cath to come over again. *Cath will probably never come back,* Eden thought. She put the bag down. *I'll have to wait until later tonight when Josh gets home.*

The sound of the front door being opening startled her. At the same time Hayden darted forward and grabbed both his dad's legs, almost bowling him over. Josh lifted his son high in the air and whizzed him down below his legs and then up again. Hayden's explosive glee filled the room.

Eden stared at her husband in amazement. "I can't believe you're here."

"Well," Josh started.

"You're an answer to prayer." She stepped forward and kissed him on the cheek. "I've got to go somewhere. I think Kimberly's lost her baby."

"Oh no."

His sympathy made the situation more real. Eden could tell she wasn't far from tears and inwardly chided herself. "I'll only be gone a little while, but I know I've got to do this."

He kissed her gently. "Don't worry about me and the kids. We'll be fine without you. Take as much time as you need."

·　·　·　·　·

Eden stood outside the ornate oak doorway with her used gift bag in hand, feeling small and wondering if she should turn around and abandon the whole idea. She noticed her soggy shoulder where she had been holding Miley moments before and the smudge of spaghetti sauce on her jeans where Hayden had rubbed his face against her after lunch. In the rush she hadn't touched up her makeup at all and felt terribly self-conscious.

I'll just write a nice note and then leave the gift. Eden had turned to walk away when the door opened, and Brent stood facing her. The look in his eyes was so poignant and pure that it reminded her of her own little son when he thought she was upset with him. She could see tears lurking on the edge of his expression and felt she would do anything to help heal the terrible injury he had obviously endured.

His voice was hoarse and came out as nothing more than a whisper. "She lost the baby this morning. She won't talk to me or even let me in the room. I don't know what to do."

Eden took tentative steps into the professionally decorated living room of white and beige with its sleek modern furniture. She tiptoed down the hall, and creaked open the bedroom door. Kimberly lay on her side with her back to the light, refusing to move despite the intrusion. The curtains were drawn, and a deadly quiet filled the room.

Eden breathed in and out, calming herself and watching Kimberly for any sign. She tried to gauge the situation, unsure of what to do. Closing her eyes, she said a silent prayer. Kimberly neither turned her head nor acknowledged her in any way, feigning sleep.

Without a sound Eden moved across the plush carpet and stood at the edge of the massive mahogany bed, pausing for only a second before climbing right in. She wiggled under the covers and scooted right up next to the tall, thin body and draped her arm gently around Kimberly's waist. The sound of the crinkling paper of the gift bag finally broke her, and Kimberly yanked away and rolled over, ready to attack. "What do you think you are doing here? I want to be alone!"

Eden thought of the great lipstick wall and shuddered. "There are some things you shouldn't do alone." Kimberly glared at her, and Eden felt she should say something but had no idea what. She smoothed the white silk duvet cover with her hand and at last simply she said, "I want to help you."

Kimberly pulled back and laughed. "How could you possibly help me? You have nothing and yet you have everything. I watch you with your kids. You have nothing to give them. You live in that dump of a house. You don't even have a degree. I mean, look at your car, and still you have them to hold and love. I could give my children anything—anything in the world, except for some reason I can't have them. My body can't do it. The doctors say I'll never be able to carry a baby to term. Can you imagine how that feels?"

"I'm so sorry, Kimberly." Eden knew that her words hadn't meant to hurt, only to push her away, but she wouldn't let that happen. Somehow, she was fortified against it.

As Kimberly lay against the pillows, Eden watched her face and could almost see her friend's feelings swirl away and melt into tears that began to dampen her cheeks. Eden hugged her, mingling their tears as they cried for far more than the loss of a small, partially formed body but for the loss of hope—for a dream that would never be.

Still, tears only last so long, and when Kimberly was spent, Eden pulled away and began rummaging through her smashed gift bag. She turned around and sat cross-legged beside Kimberly, who was still in the same position against the large down pillows, looking exhausted and empty.

"Kimberly, as I was running out the door, I saw this and thought you should have it." She held out the figurine of a little angel holding a dove in her hand. Kimberly looked at it with little interest.

"When I decided to leave school and marry Josh, my mother was furious. Her reaction tore me to pieces, making me doubt myself and the Church in ways I never expected. Then one day I saw this little statue. The faceless angel was trying to hand me peace, but I wouldn't take it. You see, I was leaving the thing that would make me feel better in the angel's hand, not taking hold and making it my own. In order to enjoy gifts from God, I realized you have to reach out and receive them."

Kimberly closed her eyes and turned her face to the wall, but Eden had more to say. "Understanding the idea didn't make things suddenly easier, but the hopelessness disappeared. It gave me enough strength to move on. I haven't even thought about it for so long." Eden's voice trailed off, filling the room with silence.

After a few moments she continued, "Kimberly, you're trying to do something so important. I know Heavenly Father will help you through this."

Rolling over, Kimberly took the gift and stared at it for a minute. Tapping on the cool ceramic with her index finger, she quivered. "That's just tripe—tripe. I may have thought that before, but not now. Eden, in my patriarchal blessing it says my most important role is to become a mother, and now it will never come true. I quit the perfect job and moved here to try to make it happen, and look at me. I'll never have what you have—never."

Eden wouldn't let her get away with that and quickly spit back, "And there are things I'll never have that you have. We both know you're brilliant and determined. I've never met someone who could accomplish anything they set their mind to, but you can. You're incredible. Have you ever thought that God gave you all those gifts for a reason?"

Kimberly held her hand against her mouth, as though she was trying to hold something back, but it wouldn't be held in. "God is also the one who didn't heal me. He's the one who allowed me to stay broken after all the priesthood blessings that said I would still have children. Just last week the bishop blessed me that I would find motherhood to be the most fulfilling career of my life, remember? I've never felt the Spirit so strongly." Kimberly closed her eyes.

"You told me," Eden whispered.

"But what I didn't tell you was that I saw two boys and a little girl—their faces were so clear. I guess it was my imagination."

Eden grabbed Kimberly's hands. "That's it. Didn't he say 'find motherhood'?"

Opening her eyes, Kimberly glared at her friend. "We've looked into adoption. The numbers are ridiculous. There are hundreds of couples for each American born baby, and the foreign adoptions are such a risk."

"So, it's going to be difficult. When did that ever stop you from anything? Kimberly, if you have actually seen the children you are meant to have, don't you think you can find them? Maybe that's why God showed them to you."

Kimberly looked at her and seemed to soften for a moment but suddenly pushed her away. "That's so easy to say. You think you have all the answers, but you can't even raise your own children. You need to leave." She covered her face. "Get out of here!"

Eden searched for what to tell her, but the room was filled with an almost tangible emptiness. She knew there was nothing more she could do. Stepping off the bed, she walked out of the room to a waiting Brent, shook her head, and wandered out into the street. It had grown cold and overcast.

Why did I go do that? Why did I think I could help her? I felt so inspired at the beginning, but in those last moments it was like standing before the ward bearing your testimony when your mind goes blank, and you don't know if you said what you were supposed to say or if you never should have gotten up there to begin with.

She kicked a rock in the road and turned to face her house. The gutter across the front porch was crusted in rusty streaks, and, from the road, she could see the dark soft evidences of wood rot inside the beam that had weakened enough to make it sag unnaturally under the weight of the roof, even with the support of the main house. The reality washed over her that the house was beyond repair. It could never be fixed. *How could I have been so wrong?*

The front door opened, and Josh stepped out with Miley cradled in the corner of his arm. Eden couldn't help but smile and feel herself drawn forward to them. But as she got closer, she could sense something wasn't right. Josh held a light blue piece of paper in his hand. His eyes met hers, but she couldn't read them. Her stomach began to ache, and she yanked the paper from his fingers and read the words. Disbelief and shock flooded over her.

"Seventy-two hours, or we lose the children?"

She collapsed on the single rickety stair, one hand still resting on the unsteady railing and the other trembling while she searched through the words, hoping to find some hidden meaning. Josh moved toward her, but she shot him a look that held him fast.

"The house was condemned before we bought it. We can fight this," he offered.

"Don't you understand?" It was clear now. "This isn't about the house. It's about me. Why didn't I believe them? Everyone close to me said it—three bad reports. How much more proof do I need?" She stood and faced her husband. "Josh, I've been pushing everyone away. My mother was right. This has all been a terrible mistake. I'm not a good mother or a good daughter. I can't do it. You never should have married me. What have I done?" She covered her face with her hands.

"Eden, what are you talking about?"

"You said it just before I left. Don't you remember your words? 'The children and I will do fine without you.' That's what you said."

"No." Josh ran to her side, but she pushed him away.

"Stop, you don't know everything. Kimberly did lose her baby, and we had a long talk. Do you know what she said to me? She said I had nothing to offer my children—nothing!"

"Eden, she was grief-stricken. It doesn't count."

"You're wrong. When we're upset, it's the one time we say exactly what we mean. All the things we have been thinking but are too afraid to face. Josh, you married the wrong person. I can't do this anymore."

"It's all right, Eden. I'll take care of everything. You don't even have to talk to them. I'll do it all," Josh said bravely.

"Don't be ridiculous. You have to go to work." Eden tried to calm herself. "It's the only thing we have left."

Josh shook his head, "Eden, the reason I'm home early is because I quit today."

Eden shook her head in disbelief and began to run. She ran up the walk to the end of the street and turned left. Sprinting past the open iron gate, she sped up the gravel driveway and threw open the door of the little garage apartment. Her hand dropped from the doorknob to her side, and she twisted around in astonishment. Everything was gone—the furniture, the paintings, and the warmth. Everything. Eden crumbled to the ground.

34

A Real Home

Y ou won't believe what she told me." Kimberly stormed from her room.

Brent's head bobbed up, and he stared at his wife, who took little notice of him and headed to the kitchen. "Try me," he finally said, following her and silently thanking Eden for whatever she did.

"She said that when the bishop said I would 'find motherhood' it meant that I had to find our kids. She said that's why I was so smart and determined, so that I'd fight through all the red tape until I found them."

"Wow, what do you think?" Brent sat at the table, holding back until he was sure which direction the conversation was going.

Kimberly flicked her black hair back from her face as she opened the cupboard and pulled out her favorite tart blackberry herbal tea. "It seems too pat an answer—like it's only two dimensional. It isn't like I should go through books of orphans and foster kids looking for their mug shots. I mean, they were American looking but that could be Western European, including some of the 'stan' countries or Canada. Do they do adoptions from Canada?"

Brent kept his lips clipped tightly together as his wife put water on to boil and walked across the room to sit across from him.

Kimberly drummed her fingers on the table. "She may be right, but I keep feeling like it will come in a totally different way that I haven't even considered yet. One thing's for sure, though . . ."

"What?"

"Starting Monday, I'm getting a job." Kimberly got up from her seat and retrieved two mugs. Brent watched her and smiled. He knew she was still carrying the grief, but for Kimberly the worst thing she could do was to sit alone and be lost in thought and sorrow. Eden had given her such a gift. She had given her a direction to throw all that emotion and through that venue, Brent knew, she could work it out. He had to call Eden and thank her, but first he knew he had to focus on his wife.

*   *   *   *   *

"Darn it!" Kevin slammed down the receiver and cupped his head in his hands just as Cath walked by the French doors to his office. She gestured if she could enter and he motioned to her.

"Now that you're bishop, I probably need to buy some curtains for those doors. You look incredibly upset. Is it something you can share?"

"I suppose. Do you know I've called every dang name on the ward list, and I can't get one family to agree to take Cory in? He has to be placed for Joe to return home, and I don't want that boy stuck in the foster care system. Can you believe this?"

"Unfortunately, I can. Their family's been in the ward a long time and created a lot of hard feelings."

"That shouldn't matter." Kevin picked up the list, reviewing the names one more time.

"There's an extra bed in Jordan's room," Cath suggested.

"If I weren't bishop, I'd take you up on that, but I think it could cause problems."

"You don't have to worry about Sandra," she said.

"It's not Sandra I'm worried about. It's the vicious gossip that's sure to erupt through the ward if we did." Kevin looked at the list again. "There has to be a better answer. I feel like I'm missing someone."

"Have you called the Halls?"

Kevin nodded.

"What about the Martins or the Kenners?" Cath sat down.

"I've tried them all." He grabbed a yellow legal pad. "At least one thing is clear.

"What's that?"

"The spiritual thought I'm giving at my first executive council meeting."

"Which is?" She waited.

"Service. Maybe if this ward would serve each other more, they could learn how to love each other more. We should develop the sort of hearts that could love and welcome anyone in our homes and lives that wants to be part of the truth."

"You're right," Cath said absently. She watched her husband scribble on the page, furiously flip through his scriptures, and write some more. She cleared her throat, wanting to say something. He didn't notice.

A little disappointed, Cath stood and walked from the room, determined to talk to him before she went to bed that night. Her stomach lurched at the thought of what his reaction might be. She swallowed and headed to the kitchen. There was still plenty of time. *This baby has waited for five years. What difference will one more day make?*

· · · · ·

The phone rang, and Hope almost didn't answer it. After her embarrassing display in front of her daughter, she was hoping for a few days to sort things out. She could hardly believe the words that had come out of her own mouth and would do anything to take them back. On the last ring before it flipped to voice mail, she picked up and, for the first time in years, didn't use her pat answer. Instead, she blurted out, "Okay, so I'm sorry."

"What? Is this Hope Lane's phone?" Josh's voice came over the line.

By the sound of his voice, she knew something was up. "Yes. Josh, what's wrong?" She covered her mouth.

The baby was crying in the background. "I think you need to get over here right away." The next three words were what Hope had been waiting to hear as long as she could remember. Josh's voice cracked as he whispered, "Eden needs you."

35

How Bad Is It Really?

Marlene was sick of Roy's badgering. So what if Cath was baby-sitting Eden's kids. They were a visiting teaching partnership, so it counted for her too. Finally, as the sun began to set, she gave in and took the flowers Roy had cut for her to bring. When at last Marlene headed down the street, it was for the sole purpose of getting away from the man.

There were no cars in the driveway, and the house seemed much too quiet. Marlene began to feel uncomfortable and glanced over her shoulder, placing an unsure foot onto the front porch. She knocked and waited. Then she peeked through the front window. There were still toys on the floor and a baby blanket draped across the old sofa. As Marlene turned to go, she noticed a paper wedged between the peeling boards beneath her and picked it up. Her eyes opened wide as she read the words. Throwing the flowers to the ground, Marlene hurried down the unsteady stairs. *I've got to tell the bishop. He'll know what to do.*

As she got to the street, Helen emerged from her front door. "We did it." Her face shone with victory.

"Helen, tell me the truth. What have you done?" Marlene hurried up beside her.

"I did exactly what we'd always planned," Helen began with her nose in the air.

Marlene glanced over Helen's shoulder through her open front door. All the blinds were drawn, and the dim room had very little

159

furniture. There was nothing on the walls. It was stark and cold. "Tell me. Where are they?"

Helen backed up a little before lifting her chin and standing her ground. "It was for their own good. That house was condemned last year, and I simply brought it to the correct authority's attention like any good citizen would. If they're responsible enough to pursue it, I'm sure they'll get their money back."

"What are you talking about?" Marlene shook a finger at Helen. "What have you done?"

"I've done what's best for the neighborhood. That's my job." Helen's words seemed to propel her forward. "I've done what should have been done months ago, and by Saturday afternoon, the subject will be closed for good. So get out of my way and go bury your head in the sand like you've always done since the day you moved in. I'm sick of you."

"What's happening on Saturday?" Marlene moved closer until she was inches from the woman.

Helen folded her arms militantly and struck a confident pose. "I'm not at liberty to say."

Marlene stared at her in utter shock and all the pieces connected. "The beautification project? Was that for this?"

"It's all perfectly legal. Residents are permitted to pay for the demolition of condemned properties, and the most poetic part of it all is that you were my largest contributor. How does that feel, making that little family homeless?"

"Why do you hate them so much?"

"This has nothing to do with them. It has to do with right and wrong. It has to do with the fact that I was promised a park there, and now it's going to happen. You see, it's not complicated."

"I do see, and let me tell you, what I'm looking at is not very pretty."

"Well, nothing can be done about it now. I've already contracted the crew who will be here bright and early Saturday morning to plow over that monstrosity. In four days I'll be able to look out my window and smile for the first time since I've moved in." Helen lifted her chin in triumph.

"We'll see about that." Marlene hurried down the street and, as an afterthought, called behind her, "A lot can happen in four days."

At that time, right down the street, Brent was juggling three heavy bags of groceries and wrestling with his keys. Finally, the key found the lock. He entered the kitchen and dropped his load on the counter. Grabbing a cantaloupe with one hand and a head of lettuce with the other, he turned to put them in the refrigerator as Kimberly entered the room. She looked beautiful. Her hair was sleek and clean, and her face shone. If it weren't for her jeans and casual blouse, he could believe she was ready to enter a corporate conference center.

"Wow, you look great." He froze in place, admiring her.

"Well, it's time for me to move on and accept what's ahead. Did you grab the paper?" She seized the sleek birch chair in front of her, slid it out, and sat at the table.

"Oh, yeah, it's right here." He set down the lettuce and plucked the plastic wrapped bundle out of one of the bags. "You should know it took the balance of a contortionist to pick it up without dropping the bags."

"Impressive." She glanced at him, slid out the paper, and let her attention turn to the pages she was rifling through. At last she found the section she was looking for and laid the page open in front of her, running her finger up and down the columns. "I might have to get some retraining. I'm not sure an MBA will be of any use in the social services field."

"Social services?" Brent tried to sound distracted, so she would keep talking.

"Yes, I'm quite sure that's the area I want to pursue. My only problem is that I know nothing about it. I'm starting from square one."

They were interrupted by the sound of someone knocking. Marlene's face suddenly appeared, pressed up against the little row of windows beside the kitchen door.

"What does she want?" Kimberly cringed while Brent hurried forward to let her in.

"Welcome. What a pleasant surprise." Brent gestured for her to enter.

Marlene rushed into the room and looked back and forth at both husband and wife. "Do either of you know what happened to Eden? It looks like they're gone. Their house has been condemned, thanks to our illustrious homeowners' president."

"Sounds like something she'd do." Kimberly folded the paper closed. "It might be a blessing in disguise. I bet they can find help now with funding their improvements—"

Marlene slapped both hands on the table. "You don't understand. Helen has already paid for demolition. In four days the house is gone. We've got to find them!"

Kimberly bit her lip and paused for a moment before saying, "If we could contact Josh's employer, we may get our quickest answer. They would know if he was taking vacation, or he may still be there. Do you know where Josh works?"

Marlene shrugged, but Brent cleared his throat. "We talked about it at the nerd party. TJ Manufacturing, I think."

Kimberly produced a cell phone from her pocket and within minutes put the phone on speaker so everyone could hear.

"TJ Manufacturing," a nasal voice answered.

"Hello, I'm calling to verify the active status of Josh Duncan's employment at your company." Kimberly sounded as though she had done this hundreds of times, which she had.

"Oh, it's so sad. He quit, and the whole place is in an uproar. We've been trying to get a hold of him. Will you see him soon?" the voice pled.

"I . . . I hope so," she faltered, not knowing what to say.

"Please have him call the office as soon as possible. It's imperative."

Kimberly hung up and looked at Brent, who turned to Marlene, and each wracked their brains for a solution. "What about his parents?" Brent asked.

Husband and wife looked to Marlene, who threw her hands in the air. "I don't know who they are. I don't know anything."

Kimberly sat at her computer. "I'll google him. It shouldn't be hard to track them down. Brent, why don't you take Marlene to City Hall and see what the legal options are at this point?"

"Great idea," Brent said, picking up the keys with Marlene following him while nodding like a bobble-head figure.

"We'll find him." Kimberly began clicking away fluently on her keyboard. "They could have simply gone on vacation, but to be safe, I'll check the local hotels and homeless shelters too. I also have a friend that may let me access recent financial transactions. Don't worry."

"I'm not," Brent said, opening the door for Marlene. Losing the baby had been hard on him too, but seeing his wife focused and involved brought a sense of normalcy that Brent had missed. Again he was grateful to the family up the street and would do anything for them.

•　•　•　•　•

Two hours later, Kimberly had learned nothing about where Eden and her family were, but she had learned intriguing details about homeless shelters. She clapped down the screen of her laptop so she wouldn't have to look at the awful reality any more. Some areas in the country were amply served by homeless shelters, but, in her conservative state, that was not the case. There was only one private home dedicated to housing the homeless in their small town. The Cochran House had eight bedrooms, but it had been full for months.

In the next city over, there was a large hotel that was open every evening but closed during the day. After reviewing the accounts of assault, drug-related crime, and unsanitary conditions, she shuddered. The phone rang, and she checked her caller ID to see who was on the line. It was the women's abuse shelter she had contacted earlier.

"Hello, this is Kimberly. Yes, I called to find out about your facility. Do you house families?"

"No, men are not allowed through our doors. We don't even have them on staff, but there are a good percentage of mothers we suspect come to the shelter under the guise of abuse when homelessness is their real issue." The director seemed grateful for a venue to vent her frustrations. "They have nowhere else to turn. It's sad that these caring mothers actually leave their husbands so their children won't be taken by the state and thrown in foster care."

"You're kidding." Kimberly listened, horrified. "Is anyone working on a solution?"

"Not really," the director continued. "The lack of facilities for homeless families in this area has seriously hampered our ability to serve our target group. But I can't see turning them away, and there is no end in sight. The government has no money, and with the economy the way it is, I don't see a private investor stepping forward anytime soon. Nonprofits are the first groups hit by a recession. There's no good answer."

Kimberly hung up and knew she had found it. This was a cause that could fill her life. This was the answer to prayers.

•   •   •   •   •

That evening, a group of ten adults crowded in the new bishop's office. Kevin had been in business meetings all day and hurried over straight from work. He had received a number of calls from Cath but figured he'd return them once ward council was over. After an opening prayer, he walked around his desk so he could be closer to those in the room.

"I heard an interesting story about a woman who hated cats," the new bishop began. "Her daughter brought home a kitten, and the woman could hardly stand to be in the same room as the creature."

"I can relate to that." Brother Harris, the high priest group leader, laughed.

"One day she went to paint her porch, and the poor thing fell in the paint bucket. She retrieved it and washed it off as best she could, but the kitten caught pneumonia and almost died. The woman nursed it for days before she knew the animal would pull through, and at the end of that time, the woman found she had changed. She loved the kitten because she had served it."

"I don't know if that would do it for me," Sister Ramsey interjected. "I still hate cats."

"The point is—" Kevin was getting frustrated. "If we reach out and serve each other more, our love for each other will increase. We will become one as a ward and as a people and will actually be what we should be, a part of Zion."

"Our home teaching stats are up this month. Is that where you're headed with this?" offered the elders quorum president.

"No, I think we need to do something more personal as a ward. Could each of you think of the families you serve and try to pinpoint someone who may need a project that multiple people could help with? Does anyone come to mind?"

"You know, our boundaries don't really include a lot of the less affluent areas in town. We don't have that much need," Brother Harris said.

Sister Ramsey raised her hand. "I've got to agree. Every sister I know of is doing pretty well. We don't even have any members in the old folks' home anymore. Maybe we could reach into the community."

Kevin looked around the room at the empty faces and wondered why he had felt so inspired about going in this direction. He lowered his head, reaching for what he should say. Then his cell phone rang. Normally, he would have let it go, but, without thinking, he flipped it open. It was Cath.

"Kevin, I'm sorry to bother you in the middle of your meeting, but this can't wait. Marlene is here and beside herself with worry. The Duncans' house has been condemned and is due to be demolished if it isn't brought up to code. There are electrical, plumbing, roofing, and lead paint problems. We can't find Eden and Josh anywhere. What should we do?"

As he hung up the phone, Kevin grinned from ear to ear. "Hey, Brother Harris, aren't you a plumber?"

"Well, if you call the owner of a chain of wholesale outlets a plumber, I guess I'm guilty," he answered defensively.

"And doesn't Brother Kessler have a roofing and sheet metal company?"

"Well, yes," the elders quorum president replied, "but he's low on work right now."

"We've got plenty of work for him. Brenda, we're going to need every available sister we can find for the next three days. We have a righteous family that needs our help."

36

Missing in Action

Dissatisfied, Cath put down the receiver. "Kevin's going to get the ward together to fix up the house, but that's only half the problem."

"I know." Marlene put a hand on her shoulder. "Where are Eden and her family? I called the police, and they won't help us. They simply called me a nosy neighbor. Can you believe it? They say without any signs of foul play, there is no case."

Sandra walked into the kitchen. "I need to use the phone." She picked it up and began punching buttons.

Cath continued her conversation. "From what you've told me, it sounds like there was plenty of foul play. Poor Eden."

"Wait." Sandra put down the receiver. "What are you talking about? Eden? Foul play?"

Marlene perked up, excited to explain it again. "This afternoon, I decided to do my visiting teaching. When I got to Eden's, the place was abandoned, and I found a notice by the door that said their house was condemned. That's when that nasty neighbor of theirs accosted me and said that she had paid to have it demolished."

"So what are we doing about it?" Sandra urged her to continue.

"Well, I ran straight over to the city hall and talked to Fran, who was in tears over the situation. She told me it was all a big mistake, but nothing can be done unless the house is brought up to code by Saturday." Marlene took a deep breath. "If we don't do something drastic, the house will be gone, and the worst part is, no one can find Josh and Eden anywhere."

"Anywhere? Did you check Josh's work?" Sandra asked.

"From what Marlene says, they called, and Brother Duncan quit. We don't know what to think." Cath's hands were shaking.

"Kimberly even called the homeless shelters and both of their families. Eden's mother isn't answering her cell phone for some reason, but Josh's family knows nothing at all," Marlene added.

Sandra touched her mom's arm. "Could we pray for them at least?"

Cath clutched her daughter in her arms. "You bet we can."

· · · · ·

Eden lay alone in bed with the curtains drawn and threw a pillow over her head to try to block out the sounds of people talking in the other room. The door creaked open, and between sandwiched pillows, she mumbled, "Josh, is it you?"

"No, it's me."

Eden sat up. "Mom?"

"I'll leave if you don't feel up to it." She turned back to the door.

"No, come in. I'm almost ready to get up." Eden leaned back, realizing again how horrible she felt.

"We've got the cabin for a week, so don't feel like you have to hurry. You've had it tough lately." Her mom sat at the foot of the bed.

"That's an understatement." Eden smoothed out the blankets across her legs and gave a weak laugh.

"Well, what I wanted to tell you is that there'll be no problem getting this cleaned up in court. If title insurance doesn't cover it, disclosure laws should."

"Mom, I don't care about the house." Eden let out a long sigh.

"What? Now you're being silly." Hope shook her teased mane.

"No. I've been silly for a long time but not now. You know what you said about me not thinking you were good enough and everything?"

Hope Lane brushed off the shoulder of her sage cotton jacket with the back of her hand. "I've been trying to forget about that and move on."

"You shouldn't." Eden sat up on her knees. "You were absolutely right. I don't know when it started, but it's like I've been walking around all the time thinking nothing's good enough—my children, my husband, my friends—even me."

"But you do know the house isn't good enough, right? I mean, it's been condemned," Hope added.

"Yeah, and the funny thing is that it was the only thing I clung on to. Mom, I've got to stop looking at everything that's wrong with my life and start enjoying the good parts, and that starts with you."

"Me?" Hope smiled.

"You've been a great mom. You've worked hard and always been there. I know I haven't told you often enough, but I will from now on. I want us to be closer." Eden hugged her.

"That's sweet. I'll try harder too." Her mom patted her arm awkwardly in response.

"Mama!" Hayden ran through the open door and jumped up in Hope's lap.

Hope clamped her fingers over her nose. "Someone's in need of a serious diaper change, and to show you I'm turning over a new leaf, I'll help." She encouraged the toddler toward his mother and headed for the door. "I'll get the air freshener."

37
Painting a Clear Picture

Sunrises thrilled Isa. They were like a great secret shared only by the few individuals brave enough to face the wee hours of the morning. Sunsets were so cliché; nearly everyone saw them, but sunrises were something special. She stared at the brilliant colors with a great sense of satisfaction. Today marked an end and a beginning, and she wanted to relish both.

Last night she had painted in her new studio straight through the witching hours, finishing her last creation of the set she had been working on since the previous winter. It was by far her best and wisest piece ever. She couldn't wait to show Eden. It illustrated everything she had learned and carried with her to this new place. The large window framed the vibrant gift of nature, Gwen's garden, and Isa laughed out loud. *It's like waking up to a new life.*

The teakettle whistle shook her back to reality, and Isa was hurrying to the kitchen when she heard a knock on the door. There stood an earthy-looking man with a fashionable older woman. Isa thought she had seen them before. "Can I help you?"

The man smiled and said, "Yes, we're friends of the Duncans and were wondering if you knew where they took themselves off to. Did Eden say they were goin' on a trip or somethin'?"

"I haven't spoken to them for about a week. The sale of the house whizzed by like silk across glass. Since the move I've been working nonstop on my latest project, but it's done, and it's glorious."

"To be honest, we really don't care." Marlene scowled. "We need to find Eden, so if she calls you, catch me on my cell immediately." She handed Isa a business card. "Let's go, Roy."

Isa stared at her. "Are you sure they're gone?" Her face was bathed in disappointment.

Marlene nodded. "The house looks nearly empty, and through the children's bedroom window, we could see the dresser drawers still open like they left in a hurry."

"It don't make a lick of sense, does it?" Roy added.

"No." Isa tapped her chin with a paint covered finger. "Is there anything I can do to help?"

"A bunch of people are meeting at the house in the next hour or so to work on the roof, clean up the inside, and paint the whole thing. You're welcome to come." Roy gave a sympathetic grin.

"Paint." Isa's eyes brightened. "That's my specialty."

38
Minor Miracles

By the time Kimberly arrived at Eden's house, it was a buzz of activity. She had spent the wee hours of the morning continuing the search for Eden's whereabouts, but was at a standstill until her message was returned from Eden's mother's office. Apparently, Hope Lane had notified her office that she would be out for a few days. That alleviated Kimberly's concerns somewhat, but she was a bit hesitant about proceeding with the project without specific permission. But what else could they do?

Three men were walking around on the roof. At least fifteen more were stomping around the outside while various ladies zipped in and out the front door, piling all the smaller household items neatly in the garage.

Kimberly searched around for the bishop and decided he must be at the center of a growing huddle of men in the back. Voices were flaring, and she wondered what could be going on.

"Okay, we need dry scrapers, tarps, scaffolding, belt sanders, heat guns, and at least four weeks—and that's just to take care of the lead paint. We should all go home now and let it be plowed." The man's face was red, and Kimberly knew the type—always looking for an easy way out, and he thought he'd found it.

She ignored him completely and shouldered her way through the crowd. "Bishop, the latest studies suggest that lead paint removal is highly unsafe and not cost effective. We can encapsulate it for a fraction of the cost."

"And who do you think you are?" Joe Jacobs demanded.

She turned her back to him and continued. "I've got something here that might interest you. A few weeks ago Eden and I got together and went through the entire property. Here is a list of each of the necessary improvements we identified."

"A wish list is more like it. That's useless." The burly man scowled and folded his arms together as though his word should be law.

"Brother Jacobs, I appreciate your input, but let's listen to what she has to say."

"Wait, so you're Cory's dad?" Kimberly asked, just realizing the connection.

"Yeah, the kid's no good, just like his brother." He wiped his nose with his thumb and turned his head away.

Kimberly decided to use the moment to her advantage and pulled a navy binder from her shoulder bag. "I researched the current code and footnoted it below. Structurally, the house is adequate. It looks like lead paint is our biggest issue. The problem with this gentleman's plan is that it would fill the air with lead dust, causing greater contamination."

"So what do you suggest, Miss Smartie Pants?"

"Joe, please," the bishop warned.

Kimberly turned to the group. "Encapsulation is the process of spreading a thick primer over the current lead paint and then siding over that. We don't even need to scrape. This may also save the window casings, although realistically most of the windows should be replaced."

"Yeah," Brother Jacobs said for the sake of everyone around him. "You think you're so good, but has anyone here done anything like this before? No. By the time you locate the supplies it could take weeks."

"Actually, I called New Line, Inc., this morning, and they said that they could have everything here by noon and would be willing to half our costs if we mention their name in the special interest newspaper article that will be coming out at the conclusion of the project. All they need is our tax exemption number."

"Bishop, are you going to listen to this skirt? We've had years of construction experience between us, and what is she? Some little homemaker? Go back to your kids. I can hear 'em crying for you." He made the sound of a baby crying and contorted his face hideously.

Kimberly's heart raced at his words, and she balled her fists and willed herself not to haul out and strike the man.

He put his face inches from her and growled. "Or better yet, go grab a bottle of Windex and do what you were made for—clean up and shut up."

"That's enough, Joe." The bishop continued looking through the pages of clean data and smiled. "This is amazing, Kimberly. I think we've just found our general contractor, if you're willing to accept the job."

"You've got to be kidding?" Joe exploded. "If you're going to be that stupid, you deserve what you get. I'm outta here, and anyone with half a brain will go with me." He yanked off the tool belt he had on and threw it down, scattering nails in all directions. Then he marched off, hopped in his truck, and peeled out.

"I think Kimberly's a great choice," Brother Harris said, laughing. "She's already removed our biggest obstacle."

"No wonder Zee ran away," another man said softly.

Kimberly looked around her. "Bishop, I'd be honored to take this on, thank you. The first thing we need is a list of everyone here and their areas of expertise. Brother Harris, if you would organize the men out here, I'll take care of the volunteers inside." She pulled two clipboards out of her shoulder bag, handed one to him, and walked purposefully around the corner with the other.

The bishop smiled. "Brethren, I think we just witnessed a miracle."

39
Revelations through Service

The turnout had been amazing. Over the last two days most of the ward had shown up for a portion of the time, and some, like Cath's husband, for every minute. Young mothers had organized playgroups so they could go in shifts and help. Many men had taken vacation days. Various others sacrificed their lunch hours or came right after work and helped late into the evening.

The sun hung low in the sky by the time Cath and her children turned down the road to Timberlake Estates. They had intended to come right after school, but Jordan had football practice and Carson was staying after school for a science fair project. Sandra was no help at all and spent the afternoon yelling at her brothers to hurry or blaming them for taking so long until the whole car was a screaming fest.

Luckily, no one had overheard the tirade because the only place to park was half a block away, directly across from Marlene's house. The kids ran ahead as Cath sat behind the wheel, enjoying the peace and quiet of an empty car. Something else had been on her mind. *Maybe if I could pull Kevin into a corner, we could talk for a few minutes at Eden's house. I mean, how long does it take to say, "I think we need to have another baby?"*

As she opened her car door, Cath noticed Marlene shaking hands with a neighbor two houses up the street and walked briskly toward her. "Marlene, what have you been up to?"

"It's sort of a secret, so don't tell Kimberly, but I think you'll be proud." Marlene winked and Cath couldn't remember seeing the woman so happy.

"Why don't you walk up to Eden's house with me and tell me on the way?" Cath said hopefully.

"No, Friday is city council, and I have a few more things to take care of before the meeting tomorrow."

Cath scratched her head as she watched Marlene leave. Then she turned and began walking up the car-lined street to Eden's house. It looked like a disaster. Roy's tractor was still tied to the massive pile of twisted splintered boards that used to be the front porch. An industrial-sized dumpster took up half the front yard, and kids of every age were dragging over the broken pieces of rotted wood and chucking them in.

The roof had been totally stripped and covered with tar paper. A long bucket brigade passed the heavy packets of new shingles down a line and up a ladder where they were being laid in a dotted pattern across the roof, in preparation for being stapled in place. Kimberly sat at a table out on the front lawn, surrounded by cans of paint, various boxes, silver piping, and spools of wire, as well as a constant stream of people coming and going. Cath could hear a phone ringing loudly and watched Kimberly look at the caller ID on her cell and slam it down on the desk, before handing two cans and paintbrushes to the waiting volunteers and giving them instructions.

Cath smiled. She knew if it wasn't for Kimberly's managerial skills and the list she'd produced almost out of nowhere, they never could have done this. "So what can I do to help?"

"Oh, Cath." Kimberly stood from her chair and walked over to her. "You're timing is impeccable. We're just about to take a break." The phone on the desk started ringing again. "I told that dang reporter he could come on Saturday afternoon. I don't have time to talk to him again."

"Do you want me to answer it?" Sandra stepped away from a group of friends she'd been chatting with. "I'm still waiting for an assignment."

"I can vouch for her. She's got plenty of phone experience," Cath couldn't help but add.

"Go ahead," Kimberly said over her shoulder. Then she turned to

Cath. "So the local deli just dropped off sandwiches because they heard what we were doing. Why don't you go find the bishop, and we'll gather everyone for a blessing on the food?"

"I'd love to." Cath ran off.

Sandra stepped forward. "I gave him an update on the number of volunteers. I estimated that there were about forty, and I only recognized about half from the church. He also wanted to know how to spell your last name. I don't know how many different ways you could spell Parker, but there you go." Sandra tried to hand the phone back to her, but Kimberly wouldn't take it.

"I'm impressed." Kimberly walked back around her desk and began checking her inventory lists. "You know what would be the best help in the world for me right now?"

"What?" Sandra pushed a blond curl behind her ear.

"If you would simply answer the phone or make calls I need. I can't tell you how grateful I'd be."

"You actually want me to talk on the phone? Sweet!"

· · · · ·

Cath found Kevin in the back of the house with a mask, shooting a clear liquid with the paint sprayer in large, even passes. Cath waved, and he nodded in reply but kept working.

"Kevin, they want to eat. Can you come and get everyone together?" Cath shouted but was barely heard over the shrill buzz of the sprayer.

"One more minute," he called through his mask and held up a single finger.

"Well." She stood behind him and tried to whisper in his ear. "I've been trying to tell you something for two days now. Can you hear me?" He nodded. Although her voice was raised, the thunderous whir of the machine seemed to hide what she was saying from the rest of the world.

Cath swallowed and guessed this was as good time as any. "Lately, I've been feeling we should have another baby."

"What?" Kevin asked, still spraying.

Cath took a deep breath and said louder, "LATELY, I THOUGHT . . ." Kevin turned off the sprayer. ". . . WE SHOULD

HAVE ANOTHER BABY!" Her words seemed to echo to the silent crowd, who were all staring in her direction.

She blushed deeply and scowled at her husband. "It's time for dinner."

He removed his mask and put down the sprayer before saying, "Sorry, it wasn't intentional." As they moved toward the milling crowd to the front of the house, he took her hand and squeezed. "By the way, I think it's a great idea."

Cath looked at him in shock. She was expecting some resistance, some acknowledgement that this was going to be a major transition in their lives, and his response was that simple? "Are you sure?" she asked.

"Absolutely." He hugged her and walked over to Kimberly to see how she wanted to run dinner.

Cath stared after him. Then she suddenly felt huge arms almost lift her off the ground.

Jordan had climbed down from the roof and was giving her a bear hug. "Hey, Mom, when's the big day? How come us kids are always the last to know?"

"Know what?" She had no idea what he was talking about.

He put her down and laughed. "You know, when my little brother or sister will be here. We could hear you on the roof. I think everyone could."

Cath shook her head and wanted to go hide. "Jordan, please tell people I was speaking hypothetically. Understand?"

"Yeah, right." Jordan gave an exaggerated wink as though he was part of some great conspiracy and ran off into the crowd.

* * * * *

As lunch ended and people began to head back to work, the sound of a siren made everyone freeze. Two uniformed officers marched across the lawn followed by a confident Helen.

"Who's in charge here?" the younger officer demanded.

Kevin stepped forward. "I'm the bishop. How can I help you?"

The older officer bowed his head slightly. "I got a call about possible trespassing. Apparently, the homeowners phoned the station and said they were out of town . . ."

"On vacation," Helen added.

"Yes," the young officer said. "They said some misguided do-good-ers were destroying their property. We're trying to get to the bottom of this."

Kimberly walked up to them. "And did they call you too, Helen?"

"Yes, they were very worried," she said officially.

"We'll have to suspend all work until we can talk to them directly," the younger officer ordered.

The bishop nodded. "I totally understand your concerns. Despite our best efforts, we haven't been able to find them, but there are exten-uating circumstances at stake here."

Sandra hurried to the group with the phone to her ear and tapped Kimberly on the arm. "I think you should take this call."

"Not now, Sandra." Kimberly's eyes darted back and forth from the officers' faces to the bishop and back to Helen. "There's a lot more going on here than you realize."

Helen stomped her foot and put her hands on her hips. "Are you going to listen to her or do your job?"

"Why not listen to me?" Isa waltzed up to the group and linked her arm in Helen's. "How are you, dear?"

Helen pulled away.

Undeterred, Isa shook hands with the older officer and smiled, her bright daisy-covered ruffles blowing in the breeze. "This is all my fault. I was the previous owner and apparently didn't give full disclosure, silly me. But maybe," she looked toward Helen, "that was because I didn't know the house was condemned. Either way, these lovely people have agreed to help me."

"I don't understand," the younger officer said and shook his head.

"You see." Isa handed him what looked like a receipt. "I stopped by my lawyers and city hall to make sure it was all legal. Here is a copy of the demolition notice, which will take place in less than forty-eight hours." She put another document in the older officer's hand. "And here is my original title, which includes this property, see? If this house is not brought up to code and ends up being destroyed tomorrow, then the property will revert to me."

"I get it." The older officer rubbed his forehead. "The owners called to stop the work, so they could get their money back. I hate it when people try to use the police force for personal disputes. Everybody, back to work!"

Helen looked around frantically and threw out her hands. "Not so fast. Everything you've said is conjecture. You still need to talk to the owner."

The younger officer wagged his head. "Good point. None of these documents give you permission to be here."

"Kimberly." Sandra stood in front of her. "Just talk to her for a second."

"Take a message," Kimberly hissed through clenched teeth and turned to the older officer. "We can't find Eden. We've looked everywhere and called everyone we know—his work, their friends, their families. No one knows where they are."

"This documentation is the best we can do," Isa pleaded.

"Wait." Kimberly crossed her arms and stared at Helen. "Doesn't the police station keep track of where all incoming calls originate from?"

The officer nodded.

"I think that information is confidential." Helen began shifting uncomfortably.

"If we could get the number where the owners called from, we might be able to locate them."

"That's a great idea!" The officer smiled. "I can't believe it didn't hit me sooner."

"Um." Helen bit her lip and slowly raised her hand. "Actually, they called from my house—right before they left town."

"And did they happen to say where they were going?" The officer folded his arms and faced her head on.

Helen shook her head and slunk back.

"What a coincidence!" Isa smiled. "Look whose name is on the demolition order. Doesn't that read Helen Murdock?" She pointed to the name on the paper the policeman beside her was still holding.

"I'm beginning to see the picture, but it still doesn't change the fact that you don't have the owner's permission to be here." He handed the documents back to Isa and turned to the bishop. "I think you people are doing a great thing. Heck, I'd help you myself if I could, but without their permission, I'm afraid I'm going to have to ask you to leave."

"Kimberly, please. It's important. She can't call you back." Sandra, almost in tears, held up the phone.

Defeated, Kimberly lifted the device to her ear. "Yes." Her voice was clipped and annoyed.

"This is Hope Lane. You've been trying to reach me?"

"It's Eden's mom!" Kimberly called out to those around her.

·　·　·　·　·

Not long after, Helen made a beeline back to her house, and the officers headed back to their car. Before the older officer got inside, he turned to the bishop. "Tell you what. I'm off duty tomorrow, and I'll see who I can round up to come and help you guys." Then he yelled over the bishop's shoulder, "Okay, everyone, back to work!"

40

All's Fair

Eden sat with her hands clasped in her lap and peered over her shoulder one more time at the crowded city hall. She didn't see anyone she recognized among the hundred or so faces that packed the filled benches. *Kimberly said she would be here.* She leaned nervously against Josh, grateful he was beside her. The children were at the cabin with her mother, which caused her a little worry, but it was drowned out by the dread of what was before her.

Her mind wandered as the monotone council discussed various issues, including new water lines, a few building repairs, and the possible annexation of a lot that would require a variance. They were the last item on the agenda. At last the mayor hit his gavel unenthusiastically on the table in front of him and read aloud the words. "Josh and Eden Duncan—clarification of building codes."

They both stood, and Josh stepped forward, straightening his tie. "We were told that we should come tonight to find out about our house. It was condemned some time last year without our knowledge. We think it's a mistake."

Eden glanced around the full room one last time. It was strange that Cath or Kimberly weren't there. They hadn't told Eden any details, only that Eden and Josh had to come immediately. She was confused and tried to focus straight ahead, hoping they would get some answers.

"I'm sorry," the mayor said. "In order to have it reversed, another inspection must be requested, and it could take a few weeks."

"We don't have a few weeks." Eden jumped to her feet.

"I'm sorry, but we don't have the power to change the codes, only to enforce them. You will have to see Fran after this meeting about getting your inspection requested."

"I've got it under control." An older woman, who must have been Fran, sat at a desk by the side of the room and winked at her.

"That's all I can do." The mayor lowered his head. "Meeting adjourned."

As the mayor stood to leave, Fran hit another gavel she had been hiding in her purse on her desk twice and stood to face the room. "It has been requested that a homeowners' meeting for Timberlake Estates be convened at this time."

Josh and Eden sat down, unsure of what to do. Perched on the front row with her neck cocked to one side, Helen Murdock glared in their direction with a triumphant grin plastered across her face. On hearing Fran's words, Helen leapt to her feet. "I object. This isn't legal. You have to have two weeks' public notice to have a special meeting."

Fran smiled and held up the bylaws. "This meeting did have two weeks' notice, and right here in section 3.4 it states that a special meeting can be held in conjunction with a town meeting if a majority of the officers agree . . ."

"Ha! Becky's out of town, and I don't agree. We are half of the board right there. Meeting adjourned," she shouted in victory.

"Not so fast." Fran pointed to the paper in her hand and began reading. "If a majority of the officers agree *or* over seventy-five percent of the association is present."

Scrunching up her face till it looked like a shriveled apple, Helen glared around the room at the full gallery and sat down.

The mayor was amused by the interplay and stayed to watch, as did the rest of the council.

Fran continued. "It has been proposed by Marlene Thomas that Helen Murdock be deposed from office due to flagrant misuse of her powers in conjunction with her dealings with Josh and Eden Duncan— and basic bad temperament. I added that part. All those for this change please raise your hand. Mayor, would you count the votes, please?"

Every hand was raised, and the mayor counted them twice before jotting down the number twenty-nine at the bottom of his agenda.

"Now, those opposed." No one raised their hands.

The mayor whispered, "Helen, you can vote for yourself."

His pity shoved her over the edge, and she turned to the people sitting in the room and gritted her teeth. "What do you think you're doing? You people don't even come to the meetings. You don't deserve a vote. Besides, who could you possibly get to replace me?"

As she spoke, a bewildered Kimberly was almost carried through the back doors by Cath, Sandra, and Marlene. Josh and Eden sat up at the sight of their friends, and Fran looked relieved. She stepped forward to take back the floor. "It is proposed that Kimberly Parker be nominated as the new homeowners' association president. All those who agree, raise your hand."

The vote was unanimous, and Kimberly blushed her thanks. Helen walked up to her. "You think this will make a difference, but it won't. All your hard work will be for nothing. Watch. You won't make it by tomorrow. There is no way, and I'll still win."

Josh and Eden rushed up to Kimberly. "What hard work? What's happening?" Their questions were almost drowned out by the chorus of voices calling, "Speech, speech, speech!"

Looking around the room at the mass of people around her, Kimberly seemed to have a light shine from her eyes and hurried to the front of the room. "Hey, people, we still have a lot that has to happen tonight. Everyone who is able to is welcome to come and help at the Duncans' house. See you there."

"What is this all about?" Eden asked.

Cath stepped forward. "It's about love. We were so worried about you. We wanted to help in some small way."

"And maybe in a big way too," Sandra added.

41

The Wrecking Ball

As they drove up the street, Eden didn't know what to say. Racks of halogen lights beamed in the dark night, brightening the left side of the house so that people could continue to put up the siding despite the hour. Its glow gave a surreal look to the house, which had been entirely transformed.

Without the dark dilapidated porch disguising its true beauty, the gleaming bay window and the fresh oak door made the house open and inviting. As she was about to step over the threshold, something caught Eden's eye, and she tiptoed carefully across the new flower bed and squatted by the front window, not believing what she had seen. A small cluster of blueberries had been painted at the corners of the window sill, accenting it. "Now it really is the Blueberry House," she whispered.

Inside, the floors were all covered with plastic sheeting spattered with paint. Half the walls had a prefinished wainscoting installed, but big boxes of it still sat unopened.

The bathroom fixtures stood in the middle of the floor, unable to be installed until the painting and paneling were complete. Eden couldn't believe her eyes and felt a new hope.

Heather from Primary came up and hugged her. "I finished the nursery. Tell Miley it was from me."

Brother Harris shook Josh's hand and promised to come back after they were done to install a new bathroom in the boiler room. Even the enclosed back porch had a gleaming flagstone floor and sported some pretty wicker furniture still wrapped in plastic.

Cath found Eden and embraced her soundly. "How we missed you. Never do that again. From now on you have the five friend rule. When you have any problem, you have to call at least five friends before you do anything. Got it? Oh, and I have to be first on the list."

Eden couldn't take her eyes off all the changes around her. "How did all this happen?"

"Well, I'd say the biggest piece of the puzzle is right behind you." Cath pointed.

Eden turned to Kimberly. "You?"

"Yup, Kimberly has been the project organizer and general slave-driver from the get go." Cath patted her on the back.

Kimberly pointed to her left. "Don't forget Sandra. If it wasn't for her catching that phone call, we would have been stopped dead in our tracks, and she's been one of our hardest workers."

"Where's the party?" Isa poked her head through the door. "I heard how the meeting went. Fran is still on cloud nine, and Eden, you nearly scared me to death." She lightly punched Eden on the arm and then turned to Kimberly. "And before I forget, I want to turn my property next door into a park since I've bought Gwen's house. Watching you here has made me confident that you're the one to do it. So, Kimberly, when we finish this project, do you want another?"

Kimberly looked concerned. "What about turning it into a shelter to help homeless families instead?" she suggested. "When I was looking for Eden, I discovered there is a real need."

"I like it! You get a project plan together, and we'll hammer out the details." Isa smiled.

"For now, the only hammering we have to do is on this wainscoting. Who's game?" Kimberly asked.

•　•　•　•　•

Eden and Cath worked together with Sandra and Kimberly beside them. They pounded away through the wee hours of the night while Isa flitted around, painting little humming birds and dragonflies on twirling sprigs of ivy around doorways, under windowsills, across the ceiling, or wherever it suited her.

Meanwhile, about a dozen men worked outside, putting up the last of the siding. At 7:00 AM the girls only had half of the master bedroom to finish when they heard the sound of metal scraping against metal. The weary workers dragged themselves outside to find a bulldozer and wrecking ball.

Helen stood beside the city inspector who wore dark glasses and a baseball cap. His expression was unreadable.

"We have permission to tear this place down. Move aside!" Helen shouted, encouraging the bulldozer driver to put his vehicle in gear.

"Wait," the inspector said, pulling off his glasses.

Helen turned to him. "This has already been paid for. You must proceed," she almost screamed.

"Not before I do another inspection." He put his glasses back on and marched forward with Helen right on his heels.

Kimberly led him through the property checklist, showing him each item that had been brought up to code. Everything looked in perfect order, and he was ready to sign the sheet when Helen ran into the room.

"I've got them. Come with me." She grabbed the city inspector's wrist and yanked him outside. "They've been pulling a fast one on you. Look." The back of the house was only half sided. "See? I told you. That is lead paint. It could kill you. You don't want to sign that paper."

"But it's been sealed." The inspector's tan face wrinkled, and he smiled. "Looks like it's all good." He signed the inspection notice with a flourish, and everyone cheered. Everyone except Helen.

"It's okay." Cath went up to her. "I heard Isa say she was going to put a park in at the end of the street."

"Really?" Helen replied hopefully.

"Sorry," Isa stepped forward. "Change of plans. We've decided to rebuild the mansion—"

"How wonderful!" Helen clapped her hands together.

"—and turn it into a shelter for homeless families," Isa added.

"No!" Helen screamed.

42

What Really Matters

Hayden sat on the bathroom counter, hitting the faucet with his mother's hairbrush. The clanging sound was almost bell-like, and Eden shrugged, doubting he was strong enough to do any real damage. The last year had brought a lot of changes, but one thing that hadn't changed was Hayden's ability to make a ruckus.

Smiling at her son, Eden whisked blush on her cheeks and dabbed on a little lip gloss. The doorbell rang, and she quickly put him on the floor before he realized that his new toy would be out of reach.

"Up, Mom, up." He raised one eyebrow and frowned.

"I'll be right back," she promised her now three-year-old and hurried to the front door to answer it.

"That's what you're wearing?" Eden's mother marched in with a large gold sequined bag over her shoulder. She was dressed entirely in black to accentuate her large gold earrings and matching medallion necklace. "Nonprofit parties are some of the most formal events in the community. Tonight is by invitation only with a very short guest list. I still don't know how you got invited."

"Just lucky, I guess." Eden kissed her mother's cheek. "Josh is on the back porch with the baby. We'll only be half an hour tops. Are you sure you don't mind watching the kids?"

"If you keep up your end of the bargain, I'll be fine. I've got quite an evening on the town planned for the two of us when you get back."

Eden smiled her thanks as they walked to the back porch with its white wicker furniture and yellow and raspberry striped cushions and blinds. Under the window was a beautiful toy box painted with wild animals on one side and butterflies on the other, a gift from Isa.

In fact everywhere she looked—at Roy's flowers, Brother Harris's light switches, Kimberly's wainscoting—she felt surrounded by the loving service of good people and dear friends. Her home had become a physical manifestation of the love of so many, and Eden reveled in it.

"Oh, there she is." Hope smiled. "My little Miley Bear." She snatched the baby from Josh and held her up. Miley giggled.

Josh grinned at the sight. "Thanks again, Hope, for that time at the cabin. You really pulled through."

"Think nothing of it, Ja—I mean, Josh. I assure you, I don't. How's work going?"

"He's doing great," Eden interjected. "They rehired him as general manager. He's divided the workforce into two shifts and got back most of the trained employees Cal fired. Last month alone they tripled production."

"That's nice." Hope smiled at the baby, not really listening, and brought Miley up close, making kissing sounds near her cheeks but without connecting. A waft of air made Hope's nose crinkle up, and she handed the baby back to Josh. "I don't do diapers."

He left to go change Miley, and Hope sat down on the sofa. "I always said this house had potential." She looked at the beautiful back lawn, which spread before them like a plush green blanket, fringed with trees. The sky was filled with an exquisite sunset. "I'm so glad you listened to my advice and got it."

"Yes, Mom." Eden stood. "I'll run and get Hayden." She stepped into the front room and stopped short. The front door was wide open. She gasped and hurried forward, looking out into the busy street as a steady stream of cars drove by, going to the party. Eden couldn't see him anywhere. She prepared to dash out the door, but she noticed something on the wall next to her—a lipstick kiss. It was only a faint mark, but so out of place on the new white paneling.

Then she looked farther down the wall. There was another and farther away, another still. She began to follow the trail, which was suspiciously only three feet off the ground. It turned into her bedroom, where she found bright red marks exploding in a clean horizontal trail for the bathroom.

As she rounded the corner, Hayden sat on the ground with her makeup bag laid open between his little straddled legs. His face was covered with lipstick all the way to his eyebrows. He sat frozen, caught in the process of covering his hands with the colorful balm. Her initial reaction was to raise her voice. Hayden sat holding his breath, looking straight at her with his cranberry-colored brows knit in anxiety.

She knelt beside him. "Hey, buddy, can you help Mom put this away?"

Eden picked up the makeup bag and dropped a tin of blush inside. Hayden threw in the lipstick. They took turns dumping the brushes and other items in the bag until everything was off the floor. Reaching high, she placed it on the very top of the cupboard behind the toilet, far out of her son's reach. Then she started running the claw-foot tub, peeled off Hayden's shirt, and called, "Josh, Mom, I think this will take a little longer than I thought!"

• • • • •

An hour later they walked into the reception area of the Garden Hill Family Hospice. The walls boasted paintings that hinted of war and sadness. Josh gazed at the tank with the lipstick tube cannon, the thorny garden, and the sad, trapped woman. He lifted one side of his face in confusion. "What's up with the neo-feminist war pictures?"

"Stop that." Eden gave a harsh whisper and punched his arm lightly. "They symbolize what brings a person to a place like this. But if you understand them, then you can work on it."

"If you say so." Josh shook his head uncertainly.

She led him down the hall to the huge two-story foyer. Large side windows showed the lighted garden, gentle flowing fishpond, and gnarled trees around them, making the room almost seem part of the outdoors. High at the center of the largest wall was a massive painting, overflowing with color, joy, and love.

It was of a mother dancing in a beautiful garden. Her happy children peeked out from the centers of flowers that enveloped her, and a gorgeous butterfly alit on her outstretched hand. The woman's hair was blowing wildly in the breeze. Her skin was fair, but it was the joy on her face that filled the room.

"Hey, it's you." Josh pointed up. "Awesome!"

Eden stared for a moment and then squeezed his hand. "I think you're right. Remember, I sat for Isa. I wonder where she is." She looked around the room and saw Sandra and Kimberly standing in a huddle and hurried over to them. "The place looks wonderful. I'm so impressed."

"Thank you." Kimberly smiled. "We used a lot of the same people that worked on your house, and it went without a hitch. Sandra here has been one of my best helpers."

The teenager showed off her new Bluetooth earpiece, which looked like something off a *Star Trek* movie. "Have phone, will travel." Sandra tapped her ear.

"It's an impressive fashion accessory, really." Eden looked around the room and back at Sandra. "Hey, where's your mom?"

"She was running late, so Kimberly said I could go with her."

From across the room, Isa noticed Eden and excused herself from the other guests. She strode over and put an arm around Eden, facing her toward the painting of the woman in the garden. "So, did you see it? Did you really see it?"

"Oh, the picture's beautiful." Eden pointed above her head. "Yes, and I'm happy."

"That's true, but there's more. Look again. It was you who helped me finally see it clearly. It doesn't matter what she's wearing, does it? Did you even notice?" Isa peered at Eden's face. "No, all you see is the love she has for everything around her. Look closer."

Eden's hand shot to her mouth and gasped. She hadn't realized it the first time. The young mother in the picture was dancing around, surrounded by thrilling beauty—that's what she had first seen. It was only after Eden had accepted all of the power and joy the picture portrayed that she noticed the young mother in the picture was wearing nothing but a bath towel.

43
Life Goes On

"ome on, Cath. We're going to miss the party," Kevin called from the bedroom.

Why had she decided to do it right then? It was impetuous, but it would only take another minute or so. "I promise I'll be right there," she answered through the bathroom door.

Sure enough, it was just as she thought. The line was blue.

Discussion Questions

1. A University of Chicago publication stated,

> *Because the face acts as a primary identification label,*
> *to cover, conceal, and disguise, it makes possible*
> *a number of acts that would usually have been out of character.*
> *Even something as mild as makeup*
> *produces a change in the person, that is,*
> *a rise in confidence that is not felt in the bare face.*

Do you agree with this statement? Why do you think this book was called "Lipstick Wars"? Is it the best title for the book?

2. Eden's loneliness makes her personal struggles more difficult. How much of her isolation is a reflection of her role as a young mother and how much is self-imposed?

3. What factors led to the "death" of the walking group? Have you been part of a small group that has fizzled out? Could it have been fixed?

4. Did you feel Helen Murdock's grievances were valid? What more could Eden have done to mollify her? What is the best way to deal with a cranky neighbor?

5. When Isa said, "Lipstick isn't a very effective weapon," what was she saying? What did you think about the symbolism of Isa's artwork? Do you agree with her conclusions?

6. Contrast Eden's parenting skills to Cath's. In what ways did each mother help her child overcome difficulties versus the child outgrowing or self-discovering their own solutions? How could each have become a better parent?

7. Eden, Cath, Kimberly, and Isa faced diverse circumstances with their own set of challenges. How did their relationships bolster and mentor each other? Did their differences lessen or increase the effectiveness of their ability to provide critical help?

8. When Kimberly was mourning about her miscarriage, Eden barges in on her. Do you think that was appropriate? Is there ever a time when someone should be compelled to accept "charity"?

9. At the onset of the story, Eden only knows one neighbor who she dislikes. How does she create a close neighborhood? Is it possible to create a feeling of neighborhood in the real world today, and why is it so important?

10. If Cath's husband and Kimberly had not come to the rescue, how would the ending of the story have changed? Would Eden be better or worse off as a result of what she experienced?

About the Author

After receiving her BA in English from Brigham Young University, Christine married Greg Thackeray and had seven beautiful children—five boys and two girls. During that time, she always maintained a love of writing and developed a phonics program used in a few local private schools. Later she authored several welcome brochures for her home town, in addition to road shows, Christmas plays, and the odd letter to the editor.

When her youngest son went to kindergarten, she began working as a market analyst, writing hundreds of pages of data. That's when she discovered her interest in publishing and decided to seriously pursue a life-long dream.

In 2007, Christine's first novel, *Crayon Messages: A Visiting Teaching Adventure*, was published. That same year Christine worked with her sister to co-author *C.S. Lewis: Latter Day Truths in Narnia*.

For Christine, writing has become a great gift that fills her days with joy and leaves her evenings available for family. It is like quilting with words.